AN INCONVENIENT OBSESSION

BY
NATASHA TATE

MILLS
BOON®

All the characters in this book have no existence outside the imagination of the author, and have no relation whatsoever to anyone bearing the same name or names. They are not even distantly inspired by any individual known or unknown to the author, and all the incidents are pure invention.

First published in Great Britain 2011
by Mills & Boon, an imprint of Harlequin (UK) Limited,
Eton House, 18-24 Paradise Road, Richmond, Surrey TW9 1SR

© Natasha Tate 2011

ISBN: 978 0 263 88666 5

Harlequin (UK) policy is to use papers that are natural, renewable and recyclable products and made from wood grown in sustainable forests. The logging and manufacturing process conform to the legal environmental regulations of the country of origin.

Printed and bound in Spain
by Blackprint CPI, Barcelona

AN
INCONVENIENT
OBSESSION

CHAPTER ONE

"SHE rejected the offer, sir."

Ethan Hardesty's head snapped up. "She?"

"Yes." His newest assistant cleared his throat and checked his notes, the nervous flutter of his hands betraying his unease. "A Ms. Cate Carrington."

Shock spiraled through Ethan's gut, threatening to upend the control he'd honed over the years. But he kept his voice even as he said, "I was unaware Franklin had retired."

"He didn't." His assistant swallowed noisily and avoided Ethan's eyes. "Mr. Carrington passed away five months ago. Of a stroke."

Beyond his recent bid for the Carrington family's island, Ethan hadn't kept up on the pompous brute who'd once been his employer. Even so, he felt a twinge of irritation that he hadn't been apprised of Carrington's death earlier. "The daughter inherited everything, I presume?"

The birdlike man nodded once before inching forward to place a manila folder on Ethan's desk. "This is all the information we could gather on her," he said, retreating to his typical deferential distance. "But you might find it of interest nonetheless."

Ethan didn't spare the folder a second glance. He didn't care to read about the happy, idyllic life he was sure Cate had led. He didn't care to learn about her picturesque estate in upstate

Vermont, or to see photos of her perfect husband and angelic, flaxen-haired children. He'd stopped caring about Cate ten years ago.

"Did Ms. Carrington indicate what her plans for the island were?"

"Yes." Ethan's assistant adjusted his weight from one foot to the other. "She plans to auction it off at the family's annual charity event."

His cheek creased in a predatory smile. "Excellent. I'll need an invitation by the end of the day."

A pained grimace crossed his employee's face. "None are available, sir. I've checked. It's a very exclusive event."

Ethan's voice and gaze were equally flat. "Is that so?"

The pained grimace tightened. "You don't honestly expect me to get you in without an invitation, do you?"

"Would you rather be fired?"

Two weeks later, Ethan's chauffeur drew to a halt outside the Carrington Industries headquarters in downtown Manhattan. Exiting the limousine, Ethan straightened his custom Brioni tuxedo and tipped his head back to survey the imposing building.

It had been ten years since he'd been here. Ten years since he'd dared to set foot in his old employer's domain. Though Ethan's own life had changed dramatically, the citadel of Carrington wealth and dominion hadn't changed at all. Its twenty-five stories of black marble, glass and steel still echoed the ruthless power of its founder and his duplicitous daughter, Cate.

A grim smile tugged at Ethan's lips as he imagined Cate's reaction to his uninvited presence, the distress she'd surely feel when she realized the boy she'd rejected as beneath her had returned. No longer the unworthy son of a laborer, a nobody who'd worked on the Carringtons' Caribbean island estate just to be near her, Ethan could now buy the Carrington holdings ten times over.

Tonight's purchase, years in the making, promised to be worth every sweat-stained cent.

Anticipation unfurled in his chest as he stepped over the threshold and entered the brightly lit lobby. Clustered just inside the imposing glass doors, dozens of New York's richest philanthropists and politicians mingled, sipping champagne and preening for each other. He scanned the crowd for Cate's distinctive platinum hair, but was soon interrupted by a knot of fawning females, eager to make the acquaintance of a new, monied man in their midst.

It's as bad as London. He tolerated the meaningless small talk and overt flirtation as he slowly made his way across the lobby. Determined to extricate himself from the crowd, he entered the lavishly decorated ballroom and wended his way through a maze of linen-draped tables. An octet of musicians played in one corner while miniature white lights and flickering candles cast shadows against the pristine cream-colored name cards.

Spotting the seat he'd finagled from a business associate, Ethan pulled out the chair and slid into his designated place. Though he'd had to trade a month's use of his yacht and agree to the sale of one of Hardesty International's subsidiary companies in exchange, he knew acquiring the island would make the sacrifice worth it.

With his father growing older by the day, Ethan's time was running out. More than anything, he wanted to gift the island to his father, to prove to him once and for all that the Hardesty men needn't scrape and bow to others simply because they'd been born poor. They had every right to reach above their station, to savor the pleasures that had previously been off-limits. Just once, before age or illness claimed his father permanently, Ethan wanted him to feel like a king, to be spoiled and pampered on the island paradise he'd always loved. Maybe then, he'd believe the Hardestys were just as good as anyone else.

The fact that Ethan would now purchase the island from the high-and-mighty Cate Carrington instead of her father simply made the transaction that much sweeter.

Ethan resumed his search for Cate, dismissing one woman after another as he hunted for the slim back of the evening's hostess. When he didn't see her, he wondered if she'd taken ill at the last moment. Not that he'd care. As long as he left in possession of the island, he'd be content.

Ten seconds later, his gut seized up in recognition and a jolt of unexpected emotion fisted within his chest.

Cate.

Standing next to an elderly socialite, Cate looked better than in any of the grainy pictures his staff's report had supplied. Dressed in a tiered concoction of greens and sea foam, her pale arms and shoulders bare beneath a fall of thick blond hair, she looked better than he remembered, better than even his most ardent fantasies had painted her. Graceful, willowy and as sleek as the horses they'd ridden in their youth, she exuded an aura of vulnerable sweetness that drew a cluster of admirers from every corner of the room.

His eyes narrowed, remembering how he'd once counted himself among their number, slavishly trailing after her in the hopes of gaining her attentions. He'd loved her then, before he learned everything about her was a lie. Before he learned that beneath the haunting beauty of her features and the innocent openness of her wide green eyes, she possessed a core of cold, heartless cruelty.

Suddenly, after more than a decade without her, he realized that he wanted more than just the Carringtons' family island. Yes, he still wanted the property for his father. But for himself? A coil of heated anticipation settled deep in his gut. For himself, he wanted *her*.

A prickling sense of unease, of being watched, had Cate turning to scan the sea of auction attendees. *It's just nerves*, she reasoned, dismissing her apprehension. Gesturing to her caterer, she indicated that it was time to bring out the desserts. Cate hadn't eaten yet, as she had been too busy making sure that those with deep pockets ended the meal with a feeling of generosity and largesse.

Unwilling to trust the details of this night to anyone else, she'd engaged the best caterer in the city, chosen all of the decor and hired every first chair the New York Philharmonic string section had to offer. And just as she'd hoped, just as she'd planned, the evening had progressed without a hitch.

All that remained was the auction.

The auction she was expected to emcee.

A twist of nervousness cinched her stomach tight and she felt her palms grow damp. She knew she should be used to her new role by now, but she still felt uncomfortable in front of crowds. With all of them staring up at her, expecting her to be the composed, entertaining and gracious president of Carrington Industries, she sometimes wished she could disappear. To become invisible the way she'd been for so many years before Father had died.

Taking a deep breath, she summoned a smile and took to the stage. She nodded to the front row of patrons, hoping they'd be too engrossed in their crème brûlée to stare at her, and began her rehearsed speech.

"Welcome, concerned New Yorkers, medical personnel, businessmen and philanthropists alike. Carrington Industries' annual charitable auction would never experience its continued success were it not for your patronage and support."

She smiled and nodded while a smattering of applause traveled across the room.

"As I'm sure you're all aware, this year we've chosen to donate all our proceeds to Manhattan Medical Center's neonatal intensive care unit. And in attendance tonight, we have the president of the MMC board and his lovely wife, Dr. and Mrs. Whitman."

The couple stood and lifted their hands in an acknowledging wave before resuming their seats.

"We are also fortunate to have multiple donations to auction off tonight, not the least of which is an antique fifteen carat diamond and platinum necklace, courtesy of Mrs. Rutherford." Cate held up the glittering piece and slowly rotated so the audience could view it. "I'd like to start the auction with her generous gift, and begin the bidding at fifty thousand."

Within moments, the bidding had risen to two hundred thousand and Cate felt her nerves start to relax. She could do this. She could get through the night without embarrassing the Carrington name. The neonatal unit would not go without its needed funding, and more babies would survive.

In no time at all, she reached the last item, the placement traditionally reserved for the Carrington donation. This year, she'd decided to gift the private island of her youth. The island held too many painful memories, and she hadn't traveled there since…well, now was not the time to revisit the past. It was time to move forward. Past time to forget.

"Our final item for the night, as I'm sure you're all aware, is the Caribbean retreat that has been in the Carrington family since 1920." She motioned for her assistant to launch the presentation. Against a backdrop of classical music, the video they'd compiled highlighted the pristine beach, the subtropical garden, the empty horse stables and paddock awaiting new stock, the main residence with its caretaker cottage and miles of calm, clear turquoise sea.

When the presentation drew to a close amid murmured exclamations, she addressed the audience yet again. "I'm confident my father would approve of having his island retreat donated to such a worthy cause, and I am humbled to be part of his mission to help those less fortunate than we. In his memory, and to help save the fragile lives that are so dependent upon us for their survival, I'd like to start the bidding at four million dollars."

"Four million, five hundred thousand," offered Mrs. Rutherford.

An elderly gentleman with a buxom brunette pressed against his side countered with, "Five million."

"Five million, one hundred thousand," called a mink-draped woman from the front row.

The spirited bidding war continued until the price had risen to seven million. At that point, the bidders had been thinned down to two. They volleyed back and forth, upping the price in increments of a hundred thousand until a deep voice from the back cut through the competition.

"Twenty-five million dollars."

Silence reigned for several suspended breaths until as one, the entire audience turned to determine who'd offered such an outrageous bid. Cate searched along with them, scanning the dim shadows along the rear of the room as speculation surged.

"Twenty-five million dollars," she repeated as she exchanged a disbelieving glance with her assistant. "Do I hear twenty-five million, one-hundred thousand?"

No one upped the bid and silence descended yet again.

"Going once." She scanned the crowd, wishing the candles and tree lighting were brighter. "Twice." One more pause as she searched the dim periphery of the crowd. "Sold to the gentleman in the rear."

Murmurs rippled through the attendees, making it difficult

for Cate's voice to be heard. "Sir," she said, leaning close to the microphone, "if you would be so kind as to come forward, I'd like to personally thank you for your support."

From the back of the room, a man unfolded his considerable length and rose to his feet. She could only make out his silhouette's profile as he moved around the tables and toward the side aisle, but something...something indefinable in his movements had her stomach quivering and the hairs on her arms standing on end.

The smooth glide of his broad shoulders, the loose-hipped momentum of his long legs and the shock of unruly black hair grazing his brow resurrected memories she'd meant to bury ages ago. Memories that snuck up on her when she couldn't sleep and was curled up alone, staring into the fire and plaguing herself with pointless what-ifs.

But it couldn't be.

Could it?

So she watched, not breathing, until he reached the end of the aisle and pivoted toward the stage. A pulse of recognition flashed through her veins and for a crazy, endless moment, time stopped.

Then he met her eyes and the past slammed back into the present, colliding against her chest with bruising clarity.

She felt her pulse everywhere: drumming in her ears, throat, head and chest. "Ethan," she whispered. The light at the edges of the room dimmed to blackness while the damaged legs she'd worked years to strengthen threatened to give way.

Panicked, she locked her knees and gripped the edges of the podium. Forcing herself to breathe, she ordered her slamming heart to calm. She would *not* collapse while all of New York society looked on. She could fake composure. She could feign cool benevolence.

Still clutching the podium's sharp edge, she mustered her

poise, feeling like a wounded butterfly caught in a net. Here on the stage, her turmoil visible to everyone, she didn't have the luxury of solitude to gather her thoughts, to corral her emotions. The only thought she could frame, her mind running in a frantic circle of panic, was *Just don't touch me. I can't touch you. I can't, can't...*

He touched her anyway, leaning to curl his fingers around her forearm while his lean body eclipsed her only avenue of escape. Her bare flesh trembled beneath the scorching press of his hand. A terrifying heat, electric and sharp, pummeled her veins, her muscles and her nerves, incapacitating her with a frantic wash of emotion that felt entirely too close to fear.

"Cate," he murmured. His voice, deep and rich and imbued with an authoritative edge it hadn't held ten years ago, sent awareness careening through her. "It's been too long."

Up close, he was even more imposing than he had seemed from afar. His features, blunt and strong, had hardened over the years. Time had honed the angles of his face: the sharp blade of nose, the distinct ridge of cheekbone and jaw. Too masculine by far, he would have appeared too harsh were it not for the tempering effect of thick black lashes and glossy waves of hair.

"Yes," she said faintly. His hand skimmed down her forearm to the bones of her wrist and hand. Limp with shock, she didn't protest as he leaned across her to thank the audience. Nor did she resist when he ushered her from the stage, steering her toward the shadowed sidelines while a thunderous swell of applause shredded what was left of her nerves.

By the time the applause died down, he'd backed her into a corner shared only by a quartet of decorated trees. He caught her other hand before she could withdraw, his eyes trapping hers with the same unrelenting command.

"I'm surprised you decided to donate the island," he said,

leaning close as if he wanted no one else to overhear. "But then again, I'd expect nothing less from a woman like you."

She reared back, reacting to the accusatory words delivered in such a low, intimate tone.

His eyelids lowered seductively. "You're too generous to allow sentimentality to override an infant's need, aren't you, Cate?"

Too stunned to answer, she searched Ethan's face for any hint of the boy she'd loved so long ago. There was none. Beneath the smooth, cultivated charm of wealth and power, no hint of his past self remained. Gone was the boy who looked as if he'd swallowed sunlight, as transparent and uncomplicated as the clear water along their beach. A stranger stood in his stead now, a hard, implacable stranger with no softness to him at all. "Why are you here?" she finally managed.

A sardonic curve lifted one side of his mouth while his eyes dipped to caress her trembling lips. "Don't you know?"

This Ethan Hardesty was polished, elegant and powerful in a way that intimidated any who dared to intercept his path. Muscles swelled against the seams of his tailored tuxedo, his laborer's shoulders and thighs brutally contained within the trappings of New York society's evening attire.

Platinum cuff links, the glint of an expensive watch and the hint of bristle beneath closely shaved skin gave him an untamed, dangerous edge that threatened to unravel her composure altogether.

"No," she whispered. She'd thought she'd never see him again. Ever. She'd sent him away, hurt him terribly and he'd left without a backward glance. "Why now?"

"To be honest, I hadn't planned to attend tonight," he said, his low voice an intimate hum against her cheek. "But then I heard you were auctioning off the island, and I couldn't resist."

Unable to bear his nearness any longer, she pulled from his grasp. "But surely you could buy any property you want."

He granted her no quarter, his gaze ensnaring hers yet again. "Yes." He smiled faintly, and it was a cold smile that didn't reach his arctic eyes. "But I thought you, of all people, would appreciate the memories I have of the place."

She swallowed, feeling the blood drain from her face. Her lips trembled as she remembered the last day they'd spent together on the island. *Their* island. The day that her world had ceased to hold any joy at all. "I don't."

"I wouldn't have thought it possible, but you're even more stunning than I remembered," he said, ignoring her reference to the past as if she hadn't even spoken. "But still no ring, I see."

Her throat tightened. She'd paid the price for her cruelty, and sabotaged her future because of it. "No."

His stare, its vivid blue clouded with a skiff of storm, flared with an emotion she couldn't read. "I can't imagine you alone."

She ducked her head to disguise the upheaval the interchange wrought, inhaling sharply before she met his eyes again. "What about you? I take it you're enjoying the life of an unattached playboy?"

Cold cynicism tugged at his mouth. "You could say it has its…perks."

His offhand comment should not have made the pulse thrum high against her throat, but it did.

"Dance with me," he said softly, extending his other hand.

She became aware of the music, of the shifting sounds of the crowd as couples abandoned their seats and moved toward the dance floor. "Thank you," she lied as she avoided his hand, "but I can't."

A black brow rose over flat, blue eyes. "I never took you for a coward, Cate."

"I'm not."

"It's just a dance." He moved closer to grip her arm just below her elbow, pressing her backward onto the edge of the polished wood floor. "For old time's sake."

She tugged against his hold as she searched for escape along the stretch of display tables at the edge of the ballroom. Finding no viable excuse to refuse him, she mustered the courage to meet his gaze and blurted, "But you hate dancing."

He stiffened, the rigid lines of his body harsh against the twinkling white lights behind him. "Do I?"

Cate swallowed, too many memories rushing to fill the excruciating silence. Memories that still held her thoughts hostage whenever she lowered her guard. Memories that no longer reflected reality. For the Ethan who'd stayed with her like a ghost, haunting her dreams with futile adolescent hopes for happiness and love, didn't exist anymore. She'd seen to that.

His expression cleared beneath a confident flash of white teeth. "A lot has changed in the last ten years, Cate. You'll find I'm not the same boy you once knew."

She stared at him, awash with a blend of both dread and fascination. Despite the risks, she wanted to hear about all the changes wrought by the years between then and now, to understand the trials and successes that had shaped him into the man he'd become. She wanted to explore the complexities of this stranger she'd sent to his fate so long ago, to test the waters of his forgiveness and to assuage the layers of her guilt. "All right," she conceded. "But just one dance. Then I have to oversee the auction payments."

The curve of his mouth hinted at the triumphant smile of his youth while he reclaimed her elbow. "Done," he promised.

With one warm palm against the small of her back, he guided her toward the center of the dance floor. She felt his heat, searing her, making her feel hot and cold all at the same time while the other patrons parted before him like supplicants before royalty.

A detached part of her brain catalogued the difference between his reception now and what it might have been had he accompanied her to the annual auction ten years ago. But then he rotated her to face him and stepped close, his thigh bumping high between hers and the wide command of his fingers against her spine claiming her full attention.

She couldn't think. Couldn't speak. The rhythmic pulse of the music throbbed through her veins, sparking along her nerve endings and electrifying her skin.

"Amazing that we still fit so well, isn't it?" Ethan's penetrating gaze remained on hers as his warm hand splayed beneath her shoulder blades. Heat licked along her nerve endings again. She sucked in a labored breath, the air heavy and thick within her lungs.

His hands against her shouldn't have fractured her breathing so completely, shouldn't have rattled her composure to the point that she swayed against him, her fingers brushing the outline of thick chest beneath smooth layers of silk and wool. But she swayed nonetheless, her legs unable to support her weight any longer.

A band of color darkened his cheekbones as he adjusted her weight against his. "You're as graceful as ever, Cate."

If he only knew. Staring into his blue eyes, she felt herself tumble headlong beneath his spell. Again. His rugged features, taut and intense, focused solely on her. His expression made her feel as though they were the only two people in the world, as though she was the only person in *his* world. The noise of tipsy auction attendees dulled and the music blurred into a steady, rhythmic thrumming that matched the tempo of her pulse.

Ethan slid his hard arm lower against her waist and hitched her up onto her toes, eliciting a jolt of pleasure when her groin aligned intimately with his. His other hand lifted hers, gentle despite the implacable hardness in his eyes, and he slowly, expertly guided her into a tight circle.

It felt right. So, so right, to be held by him. Overwhelmed, she closed her eyes and allowed the moment to wash over her, remembering the time spent together so long ago. Like listening to a song she'd once memorized and then forgot, the music they made together came filtering back, a sweet, haunting echo of the past.

When the song drew to its bittersweet end, Cate dragged her eyes open and met his unfiltered gaze. She sucked in a breath, her heart rising to slam hard against the base of her throat. For whether he'd wanted her to or not, she recognized the hatred he'd intended to conceal.

Oh, God.

She only saw it because once, she had loved him. Because once, she'd known him better than she knew herself, and he'd been unable to hide anything from her.

Now, despite the passage of time, despite the practiced mask of charm he'd donned, she could read the suppressed anger beneath his veneer of sophisticated command. She could read it in his coiled muscles and the firm grip of his hands against her back and wrist.

Just as she knew he would, he despised her for what she'd done. The emotion limned the bright blue of his eyes, creating a razor-sharp edge to his focus.

Oh, Ethan, she thought with a dizzying wave of regret. *I did it for you. Only for you.*

An innate sense of self-preservation urged her to flee, to put as much distance between them as possible. But she could hardly sprint off the dance floor, hair flying and her shoes clattering behind her. Forcing calmness, she extricated herself from his arms. "Thank you for the dance."

"It was my pleasure."

She moved subtly away from his heat. "I imagine the hospital will want to name their neonatal unit after you now."

He ignored her attempt to put space between them, reclaiming her arm and expertly leading her to the sidelines while the band launched into another number. "I didn't purchase it for them," he said once they reached the periphery of dancing couples.

She chose her words carefully as she withdrew from his touch. "Well, I sincerely hope you enjoy your new property regardless."

"Oh, I intend to," he said beneath his breath, piercing her with another inscrutable stare.

As he'd surely planned, the remark rattled her, filling her mind with visions of him exploring another woman's body on the private beach while waves lapped gently at the shore. Pain lanced her heart, lacerating her cherished memories of the two of them, together. In love.

His eyes remained unreadable while his voice deepened to a silky hum. "It's a marvelous location for creating memories, don't you think?"

Her stomach dipped as she backed away. "It certainly is."

He remained undeterred, following her despite her retreat. "Or reliving old ones."

Stumbling back, she offered a bright, brittle, *dismissive* smile. "The dance was lovely, Ethan, but I really must circulate. I'm shirking my duties as hostess."

"I'm sure they all will understand your distraction."

"Yes," she hedged. "But I can't have someone walking off with the wrong item or forgetting to leave a check in the appropriate amount."

"Let your assistant take care of it." His gaze caught hers, daring her to lie to him again. "That's why you pay her."

Cate flushed, the need to escape clamoring hard against

her chest. "She'll need my help." She staggered back an additional step, colliding with another couple. After making her embarrassed apologies, she turned to Ethan. "I can't thank you enough. Really. We all appreciate your generosity and I'll be sure to send the island paperwork to your lawyers tomorrow."

"No." He tracked her withdrawal. "I want the paperwork tonight."

Her steps stalled while her hand fluttered up to her throat. "What?"

"I'd think the twenty-five million I bid grants me a little special treatment, don't you?"

Wild panic pulsed beneath the surface of her skin. "But I don't have it here. I keep it at home, in the safe."

"Then we'll go there when you've finished up." He checked his watch. "I imagine things will wind down in a few hours, right?"

She couldn't take him to her Long Island home. She couldn't bear it. Desperate, she whirled to search for her assistant. "I'll send Janine to pick it up. She'll return before the night is over and save you the trip."

"No." He stepped close, looming over her while she made another distressed visual sweep of the ballroom. His heat burned her exposed flesh, as if she'd stepped too close to a flame. He dipped his head and his breath skimmed her ear. "We'll go together after we're done here."

A jolt of fear careened through her at the words. "No, Ethan…" She swallowed, ducking away from his nearness. "I can't. Please don't ask."

His grip upon her upper arms halted her escape. He hauled her close, his intent expression daring her to defy him. "It wasn't a question, Cate. You want my twenty-five million, we fetch the paperwork together. Tonight. Understood?"

Trapped, her heart clubbing frantically against its cage of ribs, Cate whispered, "Why are you doing this?"

His lips crooked in a lazy smile while his grip softened to a near caress, his triumph gleaming hot within his eyes. "Because I can."

Twisting free of his touch, of the domineering promise of pain in his victorious expression, Cate lurched backward. "No, you're not. You're doing this because you hate me."

CHAPTER TWO

ETHAN watched the woman who'd nearly destroyed him ten years ago, her color high and her steps unsteady as she tried to regain her composure. Seeing that he'd unnerved her, he felt a frisson of satisfaction bloom within his chest. She wasn't immune to him, no matter what she'd claimed, and he intended to use the fact to his full advantage. By week's end, he'd have her in his bed, and he'd savor every minute of his triumph over her. "Hate you?" he asked with a bland stare. "How could anyone hate you?"

"Stop it!" she hissed on a strained whisper. "I know what I did to you."

"Cate." He waited until she met his eyes and then lowered his voice to its most placating tone. "It was ten years ago. I survived." Offering her a mocking grin, he leaned forward to confide, "Some even say I've flourished."

Her eyes widened with the implications of his words, her lips dropping open into the tempting O he'd spent far too many memorable hours tracing with his fingers and tongue.

"I'm willing to let bygones be bygones." He probed her distrustful gaze, marveling anew at the juxtaposition of outer beauty and inner cruelty. "Aren't you?"

"I don't believe you," she breathed, her cheeks flaming with a distressed pink. "I was there, remember?"

He smiled grimly and raised the backs of his fingers to her cheek. "I was a boy, Cate. A deluded, naive boy."

Her emerald eyes misted with distress. "But you weren't. You were—"

"It doesn't matter," he said, cutting her off. "It's over."

"Then why are you here?" she insisted. "You could buy any island, flirt with any—"

"Cate." He pressed two fingers against her lush, pink lips while desire percolated low in his gut. "Regardless of what you might think, this has nothing to do with you or our past. I purchased the island as a gift for my father. To repay him in some small way for all he has done for me over the years."

Looking chastened, and maybe even a little embarrassed, Cate flushed. "Oh."

"Yes. Oh."

She withdrew, biting her lower lip while avoiding his eyes. "Well. That's good, then. I'm glad it will be going to him."

"As am I."

"How is he? Your father, I mean?"

"The same as always," he said. "A bit older, of course, but still crotchety as hell."

The barest hint of a smile flirted with the corners of her mouth. "I always liked that about him," she said. "There was never any pretense with him."

"Still isn't," Ethan agreed. "Dad doesn't talk much, but when he does, he tells you the truth as he sees it."

The comment seemed to relax her, as her features softened even more. "I still remember how he used to scold me. You'd have thought I was *his* child instead of Father's."

"He took his caretaking duties very seriously."

"Yes. But he was in charge of the horses and the grounds. Not me."

"Well, *somebody* had to corral you to keep you safe. We all knew you ran circles around poor Mrs. Bartholomew."

"What do you mean, *poor* Mrs. Bartholomew? She adored me."

"Spoiled you rotten is more like it."

She smiled without reservation then, feigned pique and humor blending within the green depths of her gaze. "I was *not* spoiled."

A lifted shoulder refuted the statement. "Indulged, then."

She hiked her little chin, just as she had as a child. "I prefer to think of it as loved."

Oh, yes, Cate. You know all about that, don't you? "Either way, you were more than she could handle."

"Your father seemed to supplement her capabilities quite well."

"Can you blame him?" Ethan asked. "You nearly gave him a heart attack when you catapulted off your horse that first day."

She gasped in mock outrage. "I never *catapulted*."

"No?" he asked with an arched brow. "What would you call it then, when you practically broke your neck cartwheeling off the back of that bucking mare?"

"Oh, I don't know. An energetic dismount, perhaps?" she asked, looking as mischievous as she had at age nine, when she was nothing but a rambunctious bundle of bony knees, shiny eyes and unkempt braids.

"A dismount," he repeated in a flat tone.

Her grin deepened. "A mutually agreed upon separation?"

"You always could spin it in your favor, couldn't you, Cate?" Fighting a reciprocal smile, he tried to reconcile the memories of the girl who'd stolen his heart with the woman who'd so callously thrown it away. How was it that she, in the space of mere minutes, could resurrect the past so easily? How was it that instead of her calculated cruelty and his anger, he was remembering her guileless smiles, her unfettered joy and the ease with which she'd befriended him despite the distance between their social classes?

"Is your father still working with horses?" she asked, drawing him back to the present.

"I haven't been able to convince him to retire, no matter how many times I've told him he doesn't have to work anymore."

A soft smile played about her mouth as she cocked her head. "I can't imagine your father living a life of leisure."

"That's why I bought the island. I figure I can fill the stables again, give him work to keep him busy, and provide him the freedom to come and go as he pleases without having to clear it with an employer first."

"I'm glad you won the bid." Genuine approval shone in her gaze. "I like to think of your father there, working on the grounds and caring for horses again."

"Yes." Between their caretaking duties and Carrington's retired show horses, Ethan and his father had been kept busy working long, grueling hours in the heat. But it had all been worth it, knowing Cate would soon arrive for her annual summer vacation. "When's the last time you visited?"

Her smile dissipated and she dropped her gaze. "I haven't been back for a long, long time."

"Why not?" Back when he'd loved her, he'd counted the days until her return, hoarding their time together like a miser hoards his coins. "I thought you loved it there."

"Just too busy, I guess," she said, her eyes shadowed by a sweep of dark lashes.

"With what? Your charities?" It had never mattered how busy Ethan was, he'd always made time for her. He'd gone without sleep, without meals, just to steal another minute with Cate. He remembered how, on moonlit nights, he'd gallop down the pristine white beach after her, watching as her hair twisted in the breeze. Ethan had always allowed her to win their clandestine races. And after he lost, he'd always paid whatever forfeit she demanded. Despite the warnings of his father, he'd always, always paid.

"Among other things," she admitted in a low voice.

At first, she'd demanded the shells he'd collected, pink and white like her skin, their smooth insides as soft and smooth as he imagined her lips to be. He'd watch her as she dipped her head to listen to the roar of the sea within their spiraled centers, his heart aching and his hands hungry to touch. To feel. "What other things?" he asked, equally softly.

"I really need to mingle with the other guests," she said, backing away and looking as if she, too, remembered the way they'd charted their future beneath the island sky. As if she, too, were remembering the way they'd moved from chaste kisses to heated explorations of each other's adolescent bodies. They'd skirted the tenuous boundaries of her virginity too many times to count while arousal roared hot and ravenous within his ears. *When we're married,* she'd promised as she arched beneath him. *When we're married, we'll make love. We'll make babies and I'll be yours in every way.*

He'd believed her. He'd believed in the future he saw through Cate's eyes, and her faith in him had shaped his goals for his life and their future. A future that fashioned them into two halves of the same whole.

It had never occurred to him that the future he planned was made of the insubstantial cobweb of dreams.

It never occurred to him that she'd lie.

But she'd broken that promise, just like she'd broken every other promise she'd made him. And he'd be damned if he allowed her to back out of another. Not when it was *he* who held the upper hand. Not when it was *he* who held the power. So he snagged her arm before she could escape into the crowd. "You won't forget about the paperwork, right?"

Her nostrils flared while her neck grew taut. Pleasure fired his veins as he saw her wrestle with her decision. "No," she acceded on a thready exhale. "I won't forget."

"Good." He checked his watch. "Shall we meet up at two?"

A worried frown marred the ivory skin of her brow as she tugged free of his grip. "Perhaps."

"Two it is, then," he said, infusing the word with just a hint of seductive intent.

"Goodbye, Ethan." She gathered her composure around her like a mantle and abandoned him with her typical grace.

He allowed her to retreat. For now. She couldn't escape him, and he'd be content to watch her squirm from a distance.

Squirming was good.

He was going to enjoy luring her close enough to crush her, until he left her trembling, vulnerable and wanting, just as she'd left him so long ago.

Still reeling from her conversation with Ethan, Cate tried to resume her duties as hostess for the fundraiser with little success. As she circulated, she found she couldn't concentrate on the conversational topics swirling about her. She didn't hear the music, she didn't taste the champagne, nor would she have noticed if the catering staff had opted to walk off with the weighty Carrington silver flatware and gold-encrusted china that had been in the family for generations.

Ethan's presence consumed her thoughts, making her poor company and causing her to lose count of how many guests she'd abandoned in midsentence.

"Cate," whispered her assistant, her eyes glinting with eager speculation. "If you need to leave early, I can finish up here."

Heat climbed Cate's cheeks. "Why on earth would I need to leave early?" Her tone, despite its bright cheerfulness, did little to disguise her jittery nerves.

Janine's brows arched high. "Ethan Hardesty just bought your island for ten times its value."

"I know. Isn't it wonderful?" Cate affected a breezy smile while ignoring the tightness in her chest. "I never dreamed we'd get twenty-five million for it."

"Cate."

Cate felt her smile wobble, but she hung on to it with a grim perkiness she didn't feel. "Yes?"

"He wants you." Janine's conspiratorial grin tugged at her mouth as she surreptitiously scanned the vibrant cluster of partiers. "He's been watching you all night."

"Oh, he has not," Cate protested, even though she knew he had. She hid her quivering lips against the rim of her champagne flute, unwilling to subject herself to Janine's perceptive observations, and took a steadying swallow. She then gestured casually toward the display of auction items. "I think we're going to surpass last year's total. What do you think?"

Cate caught sight of Ethan's profile in her peripheral vision, and Janine's reply registered as garbled white noise. She told herself to focus on the conversation, reminding herself that Ethan was just another wealthy guest at the auction.

But her feeble will proved no match for the pull of his dynamic presence. Virility oozed off of him, the aura of wealth and power and suppressed sexuality a potent combination when paired with his formal black tuxedo. Despite her best intentions, she couldn't resist stealing covert glances at his profile and the evening attire that fit him flawlessly. Its gleaming black wool, tailored to perfection, outlined broad shoulders, a muscular torso and powerful arms too tantalizing to ignore.

As if he sensed the weight of her stare, Ethan turned. His gaze caught hers, held, then flashed with raw desire. The champagne in Cate's stomach turned to liquid flames before he dragged his attention back to the woman who'd sidled close enough to press her breasts against his biceps. The jet-haired socialite, draped in a red velvet gown that plunged nearly as far in the front as in the back, glanced once at Cate before dismissing her with a smug smile.

Cate dropped her gaze to the remnants of champagne in her glass, her body humming with tension. She did not look up until she felt Janine's hand at her elbow.

"You're a way better catch. Everybody knows it."

A blush fired her cheeks. "I don't know what you're talking about."

"He's interested. Go after him. Have some fun for once."

Cate scowled. "I don't *go after* men, Janine."

"Why not?" Janine's eyes widened with the question. "You're beautiful. You're rich. You're smart. You could have anyone you wanted, if you just put yourself out there."

"No," Cate said, pulling away and squaring her shoulders. She knew from experience that she wasn't a catch. Her accident had seen to that. "Trust me. Ethan Hardesty and I...it would never work."

Small lines of confusion drew creases above Janine's brows, and she glanced back at him with a sigh. "But you so could, Cate. And he's *gorgeous*!"

"Oh, look, it's Chef Rupert," Cate interrupted. "He donated that lovely series of cooking classes that sold for twenty thousand. I can't forget to thank him before he leaves."

For the next hour or so, Cate exchanged distracted pleasantries with other attendees, smiling and chatting as if she weren't painstakingly aware of Ethan's tall figure at every moment. She felt his hot gaze on her no matter how many people clustered around him, vying for his attention.

She wished she could ignore him, but instead, she was filled with an itchy impatience to draw closer to him. The sensation converged within her blood until she became exquisitely aware of every thudding beat of her heart, every glancing touch upon her skin, every sight and sound and scent. Circulating among her guests while Ethan's eyes traced her movements made her feel disjointed, her body going through its expected motions while her insides fluttered and spun.

Within seconds of thanking the last of her auction donors, Cate turned to find Ethan before her, his unexpected proximity sending her heart to her throat. "Ethan," she gasped as she clutched her champagne flute to her chest. "You startled me!"

He ignored her distress, the backs of his fingers lifting to graze hers in a silent, uninvited toast. "Did I?"

"You know you did," she whispered, her awareness of him quickly outpacing her ability to craft polite conversation. Her guests' curious regard weighed upon her with embarrassing clarity. "And stop staring at me. It makes me uncomfortable."

Perversely, he stepped closer, trapping their hands between their bodies. "Surely you've grown accustomed to men staring at you."

Somehow, she managed to retain her balance as she stepped back and broke contact. An unwanted yearning settled low in her stomach. She wanted to touch him. Smell him. Taste him. She longed to bury her face against the side of his neck and lick the transition from smooth skin to stiff, white collar. The urge to peel off his jacket and explore every tuck and seam of his snowy white shirt before releasing its jeweled black buttons to expose his chest roared through her, silencing the chattering crowd. "They respect my boundaries," she clarified, infusing her voice with a hint of rebuke.

A sardonic grin dented his cheek as he performed a blatant perusal of her body. "What, are you worried I'll give them ideas?"

"No." Her pulse gained ground on her common sense, fluttering with heated awareness. She wanted to trace the silky strip of satin that climbed from ankle to hip, to run her hands along his hard thighs and perfectly curved buttocks. And worse, she suspected he could read her thoughts in her expression. "I'm worried you think you bid on more than the island."

His blue eyes flashed, glinting with a mocking gleam before dropping to linger at her breasts. "Maybe I did."

An intoxicating rush of desire rose in her veins, blurring her ability to form a coherent thought, and she stumbled back another step. "Ethan!"

His heated gaze caressed her shocked expression. "What?" he asked in a bland voice.

"You know what!" she sputtered, agitated arousal hitching hard within her chest.

His dark head tipped toward hers and his nostrils flared on an inhale, reminding her of a wolf who'd just caught the scent of his prey. "You're beautiful when you're flustered."

The boldness of his statement startled a gasp from her. It had been years since anyone had flirted with such outrageous intent, so long that she'd almost forgotten the heady thrill of being pursued for something other than her stock portfolio. She could almost overlook the fact that nothing could ever come of it. She could almost pretend that the past ten years had never happened. That she was still beautiful. Whole. "I'm not flustered. I'm irritated."

A seductive heat flared within his eyes and for a moment, it reminded her of the way he'd looked at her in their youth. He lifted a single finger to trace the line of her cheek, trailing dangerously close to her lips. "You forget, Catydid. I've seen you irritated, and this definitely isn't it."

Her mouth went dry and she clumsily twisted her face from his touch. The pet name he'd given her so long ago, delivered with such bewitching softness, opened channels of longing deep inside. It hinted at the intimacy they'd once shared, an intimacy she could no longer entertain. "I'm serious," she said. "Stop trying to flirt with me."

His voice was a quiet murmur. "Why should I?"

Her heart thumped within her chest, reveling in the rising challenge between them. Male against female, desire against will, past against present. The factions warred within her, filling her with anticipation and unexpected pleasure. She wanted to spar with him, to match wits against him while dodging his attempts to seduce her. She wanted the chase. To feel alive again. But she couldn't. Not with Ethan. Not with anyone. So when she finally replied, it was in a firm voice that brooked no opposition. "Because I'm not interested. Remember?"

Anger flashed beneath the surface of his sultry expression and then disappeared just as swiftly, replaced by a confident smile. Undeterred, he leaned to whisper, "Yes, I remember. Only now, I intend to change your mind."

CHAPTER THREE

"CATE." Ethan scolded her with a glance as she fabricated yet another excuse to postpone their departure. It was nearing 4:00 a.m., and he was losing his patience. "Stop dallying."

"I am not dallying," she protested, her arms piled high with empty china boxes. "We always clean up before we go home after the auction."

"We?" If she procrastinated any longer, he was going to haul her delectable little rump out to his limo by force, no matter how much she resisted. "You have staff to handle the cleanup and you know it. You do not have to be here."

"Yes, I do. I don't trust anyone to take care of the family's china." She angled an apologetic glance toward her assistant. "No offense, Janine."

Janine, looking fatigued enough to curl up on the gleaming hardwood floor, didn't seem to notice she'd just been insulted. "What?"

Ethan moved to touch the girl's slouched shoulder. "Go home," he told the weary assistant. "I'll finish up here with Cate."

"Really?" Gratitude temporarily brightened the young woman's face before she remembered her place and shot a worried glance toward her boss. "Sorry, Cate. Is that okay?"

Cate's expression telegraphed a panicked blend of irritation and worry, but she quickly masked it with a strained smile.

"Of course it is. You've gone above and beyond tonight and I've kept you far too late. Go get some rest and I'll see you tomorrow."

Janine didn't have to be told twice. Within ten seconds, she'd dumped her share of the boxes on the auction table, donned her coat and escaped the empty ballroom, leaving Cate and Ethan alone.

"That was a bit high-handed of you," Cate said, not meeting his eyes as she strode toward the auction table with her unwieldy load. "I needed her help."

Ethan tracked her from behind, watching as she balanced the empty boxes. She moved with the subdued grace of a sylph, as lissome and lithe in her evening gown and heels as she'd been in her island bikini and sandals. Just as in the past, her tempered sensuality shone through, drawing him with the magnetic power of some magical lodestone. Ethan could scarcely contain the urge to drag her off to some dark, hidden place. "It was necessary," he told her, forcing his thoughts back to the topic at hand. He relieved her of her burden and arranged the empty boxes in a line along the auction table's edge. "That poor girl didn't deserve to be caught up in your bid to avoid me."

"I'm not avoiding you," she said as she scuttled sideways, away from his touch. "I just have things to do. Important things."

He kept his scowl in check as he watched her lean to collect a stack of gold-rimmed plates. He wanted her off balance. He wanted her nervous and jittery and on edge. He wanted to burrow his fingers into the silk of her hair, drag his mouth against her satin flesh and breathe in her essence until he grew dizzy from it. "We agreed to leave at two."

"No. *You* agreed," she retorted, moving to lower the stack of plates into the box. "*I* was blackmailed. Bullied."

He arched a brow. "Everyone's been gone for over an hour,"

he said, leaning over the box toward her tipped head. "It's time."

Her eyes widened, but she stood her ground. "Says you."

"Nervous?"

She swallowed visibly. "Of course not. I just don't like leaving a job half-done."

"What else needs to be finished?"

"Besides putting away all the lights and china?" she said, then cleared her throat. "I need to lock up tonight's donations."

"So leave the lights and china. We'll lock up the money and go."

She pressed her lips into a flat line, irritation and worry fighting for dominance in her expression. "Fine."

Lifting an arm, he gestured toward the door. "Shall we?"

Cate exhaled noisily and then dipped to collect a small, black cash box from beneath the auction table where she'd locked it in a portable safe. A strand of shining hair slipped forward, brushing her gleaming shoulder and sliding to conceal her profile. With a flick of her wrist, she tucked it behind her ear and then resumed her task as if he weren't standing there, watching her.

Her unhurried actions betrayed no awareness of the time he'd already wasted, waiting for her, and he felt a surge of annoyance flare. It had always been this way: she drew him and he followed like an orphaned puppy, too caught up in his desire to please her to even care whether she ignored him or not.

He stiffened, exhaling in a slow, controlled stream. God, what was it about her? It hadn't even been a full night, and he already felt tangled up in Cate again. He bit down on his back teeth and forced his hands to relax. He didn't have to relinquish his control to her; he could simply slake his lust and be *finished* with her.

Three minutes later, after a silent ride to the top floor in an executive elevator paneled in mahogany and brass, he and Cate entered her father's office.

"I see you haven't changed a thing," Ethan said after she'd flipped on a muted lamp and moved to place the cash box on the wide, polished surface of her father's desk.

"Why would I?"

"Isn't that what females do?" Mr. Carrington's taste, as robust and pompous as that of any seasoned purveyor of horse-flesh, had left a stamp of ownership his mere death could not eclipse. Deep burgundies and greens, accented by a back-drop of Harvard plaid, dominated the space as surely as if its previous owner still lived and breathed in the oppressive office. Cate looked diminished by the overt masculinity of it somehow, as if the mere shadow of her father were enough to make her inner light wane.

"I like the room the way it is," she insisted, her small chin angled up defensively. "It makes it easier to remember him."

She said it like it was a good thing. Which it most definitely was *not*. For a moment, Ethan felt transported back in time, brought to stand as an intimidated suppliant before this very desk while a seated Carrington grilled him, upbraided him and meted out his thinly veiled threats. "I'd have thought you'd at least get rid of this picture you hate so much." He circled the desk to snag the heavy cherry frame that he'd always focused on whenever Carrington was delivering one of his diatribes.

"I don't hate it," she said, reaching for it just a second too late and missing.

"No?" Ethan smiled, tipping the picture toward the yellow lamplight. In it, a ten-year-old Cate, gap-toothed and spindly legged, clutched her first jumping ribbon to her scrawny chest while her proud father beamed from behind her shoulders. "You always told me you did."

She tried to snatch it from him, but he lifted it above her reach, realizing as he did so that she was still the perfect height. The perfect size. "It's a good one of Father," she said after another unsuccessful swipe. Giving up, she turned to spin the combination lock on the cash box while averting her gaze. "So I keep it."

"It's a good one of you, too," he told her. He gently returned the frame back to its position next to the ink blotter and traced a fingertip over her shiny ten-year-old braids. He remembered that summer, when Cate had given Ethan her cherished ribbon, telling him he was her first place best friend. He'd ached to kiss her, his heart squeezing in his adolescent chest. But he'd known she was off-limits even then. The help didn't kiss the boss's daughter. Ever. "I liked the kid in that picture."

"Meaning you don't like me now."

"I didn't say that." Though it was true. Looking back, he realized she'd been toying with him all along, wrapping him around her spoiled little finger so he'd accommodate her every whim. And he had. He'd done everything she asked and more, anything to please her. Anything to make her smile.

"You didn't have to say it," she said. "I heard it all the same."

"Are you about done, Cate?" Not wanting to sink any further into inconvenient memories, he turned to face her with his arms crossed over his chest. This place felt old. Stuffy. It brought all his youthful insecurities to light, inciting feelings he hadn't entertained for years.

As if he weren't good enough. Still.

"Give me another minute."

He rolled his shoulders, relaxed his jaw and strode toward the wall of black windows, staring sightlessly past his own reflection in the black glass. He had nothing to worry about. *He* was the one with the power now. He was the one who'd win. Hell, given time, he could see the entire Carrington building razed if he wanted, and there was nothing Cate or her father could do about it.

Irritated with himself, he turned away from the window and stared at Cate's bent head. He clasped his hands behind his back and imagined the excuses Cate would try to invoke once she'd put the money away. Would she feign fatigue? Would she look at him with those limpid green eyes and beg for respite? And would he still have to fight the urge to please her? To pull her close and vow to give her anything she wanted, anything at all, while the heat rose between them?

No. Damn it all. He wasn't here to bend to her will, to feel sorry for her, to soften. He was here to seduce her while remaining remote and aloof. He was here to show her he didn't care. That her opinion meant nothing. Nothing.

Cate's breath caught in her throat as Ethan watched her from the shadows of her father's office. His presence, coupled with his brooding, smoldering eyes, seemed to consume all the air, to lend an impossible heat to the nervous energy that had plagued her all night.

An unexpected hunger swept through her, making her mouth go dry and her fingers itch to touch his bronzed skin. She recognized the flood of desire from her youth, the wild, drunken excitement that had kept her up nights and made sleep impossible. "I'm almost done," she said, and cleared her throat. "I just need to transfer everything to the safe."

She bent down, opened the bottom right panel of the desk, then worked the combination until the safe clicked open. Stalling for time, she removed the cash and checks from the box and proceeded to sort them by denomination and donor in neat lines atop her father's desk blotter. She could feel Ethan's eyes on her as she bent to place each pile into its own spot along the safe's interior edge. Her thoughts raced and her fingers began to tremble as she reached the last pile and realized Ethan could be put off no longer.

He returned to the desk and placed a hand on its corner, his thighs perilously close to her bent head. She reared upright and he took advantage of her retreat to nudge the desk closed with his knee. The safe clicked shut with the finality of a death knell and he moved to lean against her last excuse for delay.

Trapped between his big body and her father's chair, Cate felt her options for escape dwindle to nothing.

He peered down at her, an odd flicker deepening the blue of his eyes. "You're done, Cate."

Cate stared up at him, the lamplight creating a nimbus around his head while his gaze bored into hers. She felt a tide of heat coming over her body, suffusing her skin with a tingling desire to explore the hard lines of his face. His chest. His everything. The surface of her stomach and thighs felt as if he'd breathed his hot, teasing breath over her without touching her even once. "No," she whispered.

"Yes." Ethan extended his hand and she flinched backward. Her withdrawal bumped the backs of her knees against the chair, and she wavered unsteadily, her balance as unsettled as her emotions.

Sardonic amusement tugged at his mouth as his hand darted forward, steadying her as she abruptly sat. She felt his tensile fingers grip her forearm just above the bones of her wrist. She didn't fight him, remaining pliable and biddable within his grasp, despite the maelstrom of her thoughts. Her pulse thundered beneath his thumb and she felt the brush of his pant legs against her knees. Though they remained separated by multiple layers of silk and wool, she felt swollen. Hot and aroused and scared.

"Ethan," she said desperately, easing her wrist from his grasp. "It's late. Practically morning."

"So?"

"So it's too late to drive all the way out to Long Island."

That crooked smile of his flattened and authoritative command flashed in his eyes. He obviously wasn't accustomed to being waylaid, and she felt his immutable will gather like the waves before a storm. "You honestly think that tactic will work with me?"

"It should," she blurted. "I don't know why you want to take care of it tonight, anyway. We can have our lawyers deal with all the paperwork tomorrow."

"I never delegate personal transactions to my staff."

Cate swallowed, daring to meet his eyes. "Signing papers is personal?"

His blue gaze intensified. "For the island? Yes. As I said before, the memories I have of the place are quite...charming."

A casual observer wouldn't have detected the subtext in his words, so smooth was his delivery. But she wasn't a casual observer, and they both knew it. *Charming*? she thought, her emotions a crazy blend of anguish and tortured amusement. The memories she had were anything *but* charming. They haunted her, had consumed her, had been the only thread of hope that had kept her fighting to live. To walk.

How many pain-filled days and wretched nights had those memories been her only solace? She knotted her hands in her lap. "It's been abandoned for years, you know," she told him, braving his censure as she maintained eye contact. "I can't vouch for its upkeep."

"But surely you remember that the wildness of it was my favorite part," he said in a low voice filled with promise. With danger. His long, narrow feet inched toward hers as he relaxed back against the edge of her father's desk and crossed his arms over his wide chest. She felt the heat radiating off of him. Too close. "The ripe, sultry scents. The tropical heat that made me lazy and uninhibited and...reckless."

Cate heard his memories in the words, the memories of them, together. The way they'd raced each other along the water's edge, splashing and shrieking and falling together as the waves crashed over their bodies. The way he'd trickled dry, hot sand onto her bare stomach. The way he'd painted the edges of her bikini, first with the bright flamingo lily, then with the tentative tips of his callused fingers. "Yes, well," she said at last, forcing a smile despite her nervous swallow. "It sounds like you and your father will be happy there, then."

"Happy," he repeated, his face inscrutable, but his eyes still claiming hers.

Gingerly, Cate withdrew from his heat, pressing her shoulders against the back of the chair. "Yes. You deserve happiness, and I've always hoped you'd found it."

"You," he said, the seductive note in his voice flattening to terseness, "wish me to be happy."

"Of course I do!" she insisted, thinking of their earlier friendship, the easy way they'd loved each other. She'd been happy then. They both had been, and she still grieved the aching loss of that effortless joy. "Despite everything else, you must know that I've never wanted anything but your happiness and success." She'd given up everything, *everything*, so that he could have a future.

He stared at her in silence, unmoving except for the flexing of his jaw. "Happiness is overrated," he finally said.

"You can't mean that," she whispered. She'd sacrificed too much, lost too much, and she wouldn't survive if she believed it had all been for nothing. "You can't be that bitter."

"But success?" he interrupted, reclaiming his sardonic edge of humor. "Success supplies everything a man like me could ever want." His smile didn't quite reach his eyes. "Though, to be honest, I'm not sure it's what you had in mind."

"It's not."

"Success grants me control, Cate. Power. Influence," he

said. His eyes, sharp with intent, didn't match the easy, composed tone of his voice. "It lets me get what I want, whenever I want it."

Disappointment in his hard, ruthless words tightened her features, made her tongue feel thick within her mouth. "You're not like that."

"I'm not?" Though she hadn't been aware of him shifting closer, there was no denying his sudden, looming nearness. He didn't touch her, but the solid bulk of his torso, the heat of his stare, burned her with acute intensity.

Within the protesting storm of emotions, a raw physical wanting clenched and fluttered and yearned. She went weak with the hunger to touch him, to pull his head to her breast and soothe the harshness from his brow. She shouldn't have allowed him to follow her up here, she thought wildly. She should have run from him the moment she'd left the dance floor. "Don't," she warned him feebly, her heart filling her throat.

"Don't what?" he ground out. "Buy the island? Donate money to all those helpless little babies?" His glance traced her eyes, her cheeks and her mouth, warm and close and terrifying. "Make the Carrington auction an unrivaled *success*?"

"I..." She couldn't think with him so close. Couldn't string one coherent thought together with his big body hovering so intimately over hers.

"You brought this on yourself, Cate," he told her, his icy blue gaze trapping hers. "The minute you decided to sell the island, you invited me here."

Cate forced her eyes to stay open, to remain outwardly unaffected by his outrageous words. "I did no such thing," she protested on a scandalized whisper.

"You're telling me you didn't put it up for auction because you wanted me here?"

Fire seeped into her cheeks. "Of course I didn't!"

"Ah, Catydid," he breathed, his fingers lifting to graze her cheek. "You always were a terrible liar."

A wave of wanting flooded her limbs, tugged deep within her stomach. "I don't want this, Ethan. I swear I don't."

"Too bad, sweet, because *I* do," he said, lifting hooded eyes to hers. "Only this time, I won't scurry off with my tail between my legs just because you've changed your mind about us."

Flame kissed her skin, tinged with a hint of guilt. "Ethan, I didn't…" she started, before her denial trailed off into a futile, damning silence.

His smile flashed again, predatory and triumphant. "We have unfinished business." His voice was low with soft, dangerous menace. "You know it as well as I."

"No," she managed, her heart leaping within her throat. "You said it was in the past. Surely you don't intend to pick up where we left off."

"Oh, but I do," he said quietly, his breath skimming her mouth with searing intent. "And you won't stop me, either, because you want me just as much as I want you."

"I don't," she blurted, needing to call a halt to the dizzying implications of his words. "This is crazy. *You're* crazy."

"Maybe. Maybe not."

Rational thought scattered as Ethan leaned to lift a strand of hair from her cheek. One hand braced against the arm of the chair and his knee pressed against the seam between hers. Cate felt her self-control waver, his closeness stripping her of her resistance. His scent filled her nostrils—the clean smell of his flesh, the hint of mint and cologne mixed with the warm, heady essence she'd never, ever forgotten. Inhaling deeply, the impact of his nearness jolted her on an elemental, cellular level. How could she fight him when he was so close?

Tethered to him by her own longing, she remained immobile as his knee nudged hers apart and his fingers tucked the hair behind her ear and then trailed down to the side of her neck. Before she realized the precariousness of her position, his hand cupped the back of her skull in a steady, yet gentle grip.

Too soon, she realized she hadn't even tried to resist him. Too soon, she realized her body had communicated what her mind wanted to keep hidden. Weak with excitement, desire and worry that he'd stop before he'd begun, she could only hang suspended, awaiting his next move.

"Tell me you don't want this," he breathed against the sensitive shell of her ear. Hot breath soughed over her jaw, her cheek, her mouth, and she felt her body go taut with need. The fact that she didn't fight him seemed to intensify the heat climbing between them, inflaming him. "Tell me," he demanded as drugged anticipation tipped her head back beneath his.

The memories of their shared past, of the agonizing tide of frustrated arousal and longing, consumed her in a torrent of desire, and she no longer cared about the reasons she should push him away. She couldn't think beyond now, this moment, and the feel of Ethan's hot mouth capturing hers.

His kiss began softly, drugging her senses before it transformed to a greedy, voracious sort of worship. His hot tongue delved deep inside, confident and sure, and she trembled in pleasure, her soft whimper lost beneath his questing lips.

They'd discovered kissing together, learned the nuances of mouths and tongue and arousal, and her body remembered every lesson he'd ever taught her. His lips softened as he toyed with hers, nipping at her mouth with a playful pinch of his teeth before, impatient, he resumed his aggressive exploration.

His hand pressed down between her back and the leather chair, sliding low around her ribs and then hauling her out of the seat and up against him. She arched into his heat, moaning

as he tugged her closer, grinding the hard rid
against her belly. Squirming, she lifted to h
hance their fit, and he leaned back, dragging
up until their groins aligned.

Pleasure raged, building to an almost terrifying intensity
as passion roared between them. Blind to everything but this
moment, Cate met him kiss for kiss, touch for touch, her
fingers clinging for purchase against the tight swell of his
shoulders.

But when his hand shifted to her breast, his palm grazing
its sensitive tip, she lurched sideways with a shuddering gasp.
It was too much, too soon, and her loss of control frightened
her beyond anything she could have anticipated. Disoriented
and stunned, Cate fell forward against the desk, pressing her
palms against the glossy surface. She struggled for balance
while the room spun and her legs quavered. Wracking, shuddering pulls of breath fractured the air within her lungs while
inner tumult and the annihilating pleasure of his kiss robbed
her of any coherent protest.

"Cate." His voice sounded smooth. Controlled. As if he
hadn't just eviscerated her will with one searing kiss.

She looked up to find he'd collected her coat.

He held the cream wool aloft, one black brow arched in
challenge. "My driver is waiting."

CHAPTER FOUR

ETHAN didn't remember escorting Cate outside, his banked desire urging him to seduce Cate *here, now, atop Carrington's damn desk if need be*. Somehow, his will coerced his body into submission and they arrived at his limousine without him losing all semblance of civility. He handed her onto the heated leather seat, closed the door and marshaled his teetering control with a hissing inhale. His skin hummed with awareness and the thought of two uninterrupted hours of time with Cate nearly sent him over the edge. Taking advantage of the bracing October air, he pulled in another steadying breath before opening the door and sliding in next to her.

"Long Island. The Carrington estate," he told Walter before easing back into the seat, flipping on the dome light and activating the privacy panel.

Cate watched the black panel of glass slide upward, her pulse jumping visibly against her throat. She'd plastered herself up against the door, almost as if she intended to hurl herself out to the pavement should he dare to slide close enough to touch her. Not that he blamed her. If what had happened in her office were any indication, he'd be hard-pressed to stop the raging inferno of lust that flared the moment he tasted her mouth beneath his. As it was, her scent alone, with its intoxicating undertones of vanilla and citrus, tempted him to forget finesse and take her now, against the supple leather, the consequences be damned.

But no. He intended to savor his seduction, to prolong the sweet taste of her submission before he crushed her.

"Buckle up," he told her, feigning calm as he fastened his own seat belt. "We don't want to jeopardize that beautiful neck of yours."

She started and then fumbled for the seat belt, cinching it tight across her lap. Lacing her trembling fingers together, she pressed them against the chrome buckle and then dropped her focus to the backs of her thumbs.

He allowed her the moment of retreat, using the time to adjust his plans. He'd reacted to her bewitching kiss more than he'd anticipated, while the exquisite vision of her swollen mouth, bared shoulders and the slim column of her throat merged with the worn memories of the Cate he'd once treasured. He'd meant to keep the Cate of his memories separate from the coldhearted beauty he knew her to be. The fact that kissing her had somehow blended the two didn't sit well in his gut.

The Cate of his memories didn't exist. She never had. He couldn't allow her to lull him into thinking otherwise.

He had to remember that beneath her enchanting surface lurked a cruel, vindictive liar who used men for her own desires. He couldn't allow himself to forget the way she'd used him and then discarded him.

Though time had ripened Cate's beauty to the point that just looking at her aroused him to a painful degree, he could not allow his emotions to become involved. Yes, her lush body had gained curves in the years they'd been apart, and yes, her girlish features had matured into those of a woman in her prime. But it didn't matter. She couldn't matter.

He told himself he was glad that her wide eyes, as clear as the Caribbean Sea they'd swum in as children, looked haunted now. Sad. Grief over her father's death had sculpted her face into a fragile composition of delicate cheekbones, thin wings of brow and plump, pink lips. He wanted to revel in her grief, to rejoice in her pain, but kissing her had twisted his emotions so thoroughly that he felt almost human again.

The sensation was not pleasant.

Ethan opened the side bar, poured a tumbler of Scotch and extended it toward her. "Drink?"

She shook her head without looking at him.

Undeterred, he tossed back a burning swallow.

It didn't help.

Cate's profile still drew his gaze. As he traced the shadow and light that gilded her features, he reminded himself that she hadn't married for good reason. Surely, she'd had offers. If not for her beauty, then for her wealth.

But she'd rejected them all, undoubtedly with the same cool disregard she'd shown him. She was her father's daughter, after all, and no one would ever be good enough.

He took another fiery swallow of Scotch while visions of his triumph played in his mind. Soon, he'd find his pleasure between Cate's creamy thighs, consume her cries of ecstasy and make her beg for more and more and more. And when he was done with her, when he'd exorcised her from his very bones, he would be the one to walk away. He would be the one in control.

Perhaps then, he would finally be able to destroy the memories that still arose during his unguarded moments. Perhaps then, he'd no longer see her heart-shaped mouth, her smooth brow, or the satiny curve of her cheek in the faces of nameless strangers. Perhaps then, he'd finally see she was just like every other female he'd met. Shallow. Forgettable. Interchangeable.

Once he'd satisfied the inconvenient desire for Cate, once he'd dispelled all traces of his adolescent dreams of animal pleasure, he could finally claim a measure of peace. He didn't fool himself into thinking he'd find happiness. He certainly didn't want love. Hell, he'd given up believing in such illusions years ago. No, it would be enough just to rid himself of her, and to prove, once and for all, that she meant nothing to him.

They rode for several miles before Ethan's voice interrupted her thoughts. "So tell me, Cate, why haven't I seen you on the dressage circuit lately?"

She dared a glance at him, finding his eyes unreadable and remote. She didn't trust his expression. Didn't trust his motives. How could he have kissed her so thoroughly and not be affected? Looking at him, at his expectant expression, it was as if the kiss had never happened.

Yet she still felt the memory of his touch humming against her skin. She could *feel* the banked arousal simmering beneath the surface, sparking in the air between them. It made her uneasy. And she didn't know how to navigate the minefield of the past without revealing her susceptibility to him. "I don't compete anymore," she finally said.

"No?" He arched a disbelieving brow. "But horses and riding were your life."

You were my life. "I developed other interests," she said with a noncommittal shrug.

His eyes narrowed, assessing. "It was because of your accident, wasn't it?"

"What?" she blurted.

"Your accident," he said softly. "That's why you stopped riding."

"How do you know about that?" *What else did he know? Oh, God, what if he knew?*

"I understand it was touch and go for a while there, that you were lucky to have survived, let alone—"

"I don't know who supplied your information," she interrupted. "But they exaggerated." Forcing lightness, she swept a hand over her once-crippled legs. She couldn't bear it if he knew about her damaged body and the scars that would forever handicap her future. She couldn't bear his pity. "As you can see, I'm fine. No worse for the wear."

"But you stopped riding."

"I don't like riding anymore."

A low rumble of laughter filled the air between them. "You. Don't like riding."

She bristled beneath his sarcastic tone. "Why is that so hard to believe?"

A cocked ebony brow told her all she needed to know. "You're not a quitter, Cate."

"Spare me," she warned with a huff of breath. "Father spent the last nine years of his life delivering variations on the whole 'get back on the horse' lecture. I'm immune to it."

He inclined his head, a subtle sign of reluctant acquiescence. "All right, then. We won't talk about your sudden aversion for the horses you once loved. Why don't you tell me about the men you've dated instead?"

Before she could stop it, a startled laugh erupted from her throat. "Me? Dating? Ethan, if your sources were any good, you'd know the answer to that already."

His gaze intensified. "You're right. Maybe I should have asked why you haven't dated anyone seriously." His expression turned dangerous. Seductive and sultry as his voice dipped low. "Have you been waiting for my return?"

She averted her eyes while the truth curled within her stomach. "Of course not."

"Then why have you denied all the men who've pursued you? Surely there was a decent one somewhere in the bunch."

"I got tired of competing with my stock portfolio for a

man's attention." She softened the bitter statement with a flutter of her hand. "It's much easier to avoid the whole dating scene altogether than to try to divine a man's true motives."

"You could always date a rich man." He slanted her a smoldering glance, warming to the idea. "A man like me, for instance."

She laughed nervously at that, shaking her head. "Subtle. It's a wonder you and your ego can both fit in the same car."

"We've come to an agreement, he and I." His eyes glinted with focused intent, heating her despite her efforts to keep the conversation light. "I get him what he wants—you, namely—and he leaves me alone."

"Let me guess. You learned these outrageous flirting techniques from all those supermodels, didn't you?"

The glint in his eyes turned feral. "Cate Carrington, have you been keeping tabs on me?"

A blush blossomed in her chest and quickly burned a path to her hairline. "No. But I'd have to be both blind and stupid not to notice that you're the featured real estate mogul in every other issue of the gossip magazines."

Her denial seemed to amuse him, as if he somehow acknowledged her lie and was willing to tolerate it. For now. "Yet you accuse my sources of exaggerating," he said, leaning forward to trace a finger along her upper arm.

She withdrew from his touch, her stomach trembling at his nearness. "Not all pictures lie."

He watched her, his beautiful mouth crooked in an unnerving smile. "What can I say? I took a gamble on the American Dream and it paid off. In Europe." His intent gaze held too much confident prowess to put her at ease. "Can I help it if my success attracts tall, leggy brunettes?"

Cate swallowed, shifting her thigh away from contact with his splayed hand. "I can see it's a real trial for you, juggling so much female attention along with the demands of business."

"Yes, well, I *do* have good employees who are able to pick up the slack on occasion."

"Did any of them come to New York with you?"

"You mean besides my entourage of models?" he asked with a sarcastic tilt to his lips.

She shot him a speaking glance. "They're not your employees."

"A couple of them actually are," he said. "But to answer your question, yes. I brought a team of twelve while we do some scouting for new properties. But we won't be here for long."

"Not enough interesting properties here in the States?"

"Not at all. There are plenty. But as talented as my board of directors and developers in Europe are, I still have to be on site for the big decisions."

"Of course you do." She cocked her head. "You don't relinquish control to anyone, do you?"

"What successful businessman does?"

She acknowledged his point with a nod.

"Even with the right people on a team, bringing different strengths and resources to the table, there will always be a need for leadership."

Cate studied his face, trying to understand the gradual transformation that had turned the boy she'd loved into the successful, driven man seated beside her. "You're a good leader, aren't you?"

His white, predator's teeth flashed. "Depends. According to some, yes. But to others, I'm a manipulative, domineering bastard."

"You?" She arched an amused brow. "Never."

They exchanged a smile, a smile that didn't seem underscored by defensiveness or anger, and Cate felt a small glow of happiness collect in her chest. "I always knew you'd do well, Ethan."

His smile lost its moorings. "Really."

She nodded while her stomach fluttered with nerves. "That's why I did it, you know."

"It?" he clarified, his mouth now a grim line.

Biting her bottom lip, she dared to meet his eye. "Sent you away."

Anger slammed back into his expression as quickly as it had disappeared, burning like live coals within the brittle blue of his eyes. "I don't want to discuss the past."

"I know it's uncomfortable. But I want you to know my reasons."

"Why?"

"Because I've missed your friendship. I've missed the honesty we used to share." She felt herself flush, but continued. "I hated lying to you, and I've always felt guilty about the awful things I said."

He stared at her for a long moment, then offered a faint, chilling smile. "Really."

CHAPTER FIVE

"YES." Cate inhaled a bracing lungful of air, nervous now that the opportunity to unburden the lies of her past was here. "You can't know how wretched I've felt, how many times I've wished there could have been another way."

He simply looked at her, his expression impossible to read.

"When I told you I didn't want you anymore, I lied. You were my best friend. Losing you was the hardest thing I've ever endured. You have to believe that."

A slow blink revealed nothing of his thoughts. "Do I?"

Heat climbed her chest, but she barreled through the confession. "The only reason I did what I did was because I wanted you to reach your potential instead of languishing on the island, waiting for my next vacation. I wanted you to take your job offer, make connections and build a future for yourself. I couldn't have lived with myself if I'd allowed you to sacrifice everything to stay with me."

His expression didn't change, though a small muscle ticked in his jaw. "So you weren't just toying with an underling, slumming with the help until you found somebody better."

Guilt twisted mercilessly in her belly and she dropped her gaze to her lap. "I only said that because I couldn't think of another way to convince you to leave," she mumbled.

"Because you thought I'd have languished, had I stayed."

"Was I wrong?" She bit her lip and then lifted her gaze. "I knew you'd choose me over your ambition, given the choice."

"Now who's got the ego?"

"I know. I'm sorry." She twisted her hands in her lap, willing him to understand. "But whether I was right or not, that's what I believed at the time." Closing her eyes, she inhaled once again for courage. "I lied based on that belief. I lied so you'd take the internship my father had arranged."

"The internship?" His voice was low. Dangerous and very, very controlled.

A thread of nervousness snaked down Cate's spine. "Yes. Your internship with Stevenson and Sons. Father arranged it on the condition that I break things off with you."

His eyes narrowed the merest fraction of an inch. "He blackmailed you with a job for me?"

"No!" She grimaced. "Well, kind of. But not really. He just made it easier for me to make the right decision. We both knew you'd only have a future if you left the estate, and by your own admission, you wouldn't have left without me forcing you to."

"So I was your charity case."

"Of course you weren't! I just wanted you to be happy. Successful. And I knew if you stayed, you'd end up being neither." She clamped her hands together and leaned toward him. "I only sent you away because I felt like I had no choice. I didn't want you to look back on your life later and resent me."

His eyes flashed blue fire. "Why thank you, Cate. Thank you for paving the way to my future with your rejection."

Her stomach quailed at the coldness in his tone. "It hurt me, too."

"I imagine it did."

"You don't sound like you believe me."

His mouth smiled, though nothing else did. "Why wouldn't I, when your sacrifice helped make me into such a raging success?"

"You look angry."

His expression softened as if he'd flipped a switch, trading rage for sensuality within the blink of an eye. "I'm not angry, Cate. I'm grateful. Appreciative." He reached over to tuck a strand of hair behind her ear. "Here all this time, I've thought you were just the reason for my childhood happiness, yet it turns out you're the reason for everything."

"I didn't tell you because I wanted your gratitude."

"Shh. Don't be modest." His voice caressed her as smoothly as that single finger drifting down the side of her neck. "You'll spoil it."

She shook her head, feeling inexplicably off kilter. "But—"

"I listened to your confession." His eyes dared her to speak again. "Let that be enough."

Twenty minutes of tension-filled silence later, Ethan's driver pulled into her Cold Spring Harbor estate. The wheels of Ethan's limousine crunched over autumn leaves and the eastern sky showed hints of dawn as the sun crept toward the horizon. Cate's nerves jumped when the driver cut the engine, plunging them into an even heavier silence.

Without conversation to distract her, she'd had too much time to think about all the things she neglected to say, about the parts of the truth she'd kept from him. She closed her eyes, willing the memories away. Things were different now. *They* were different. The love she'd felt for him in the past did not have a place in her future.

"It looks smaller than I remember," Ethan said, leaning forward to look at the muted landscape lighting and dual colonial columns of the Carrington mansion.

Grateful for the innocuous topic, Cate offered a nervous smile. "I've heard that happens."

Ethan opened his door just as his chauffeur opened Cate's. A brisk breeze from the shore lifted the ends of her hair and a small torrent of leaves spun into the car. She shivered, then turned to accept the chauffeur's extended hand. "Thank you," she told him, stretching to a stand on the cobbled brick driveway and then tightening her coat about her waist. "Would you like to come inside for some coffee?" she offered.

The chauffeur exchanged a glance with Ethan and shook his head. "No, thank you, ma'am. I'll be fine out here."

"It's really no bother," she insisted.

Ethan stepped close, leaning to speak softly against her hair. "Walter knows I've waited all night to be alone with you. He doesn't wish to intrude."

Shivers rippled out from the epicenter of his grazing touch, and suddenly, she didn't know where to rest her gaze.

Mercifully, the uniformed driver avoided her eyes as he tipped his hat and then circled the car to resume his seat behind the wheel. Too soon, Cate and Ethan were left alone in the predawn dark, the muted garden lights and pale blue dash lights of the limousine their only illumination. Cate swallowed, nervousness bringing a tingle of dampness to her palms.

Ethan's hand settled against her spine. "Can you see well enough to navigate in those shoes?"

"I'm fine," she said, twisting away from him until a sliver of air separated them.

He followed her as she scurried toward the wide porch. The click of her heels against the pine steps sounded as panicked as she felt, and she wondered if he noticed her agitation.

Drawing up behind her, his broad chest skimming her shoulder blades, he leaned over her neck and asked in a deep voice, "You running from something, Catydid?"

"Of course not," she lied. She fumbled with her clutch, and her keys clattered to the wooden planks beneath her feet.

"Allow me." He squatted to retrieve her keys and then straightened by incremental degrees, his shadowed gaze tracking every trembling inch of her body. Brushing her nerveless hand aside, he fit the key in the lock and turned it with a soft click. They stood in breathless silence for several excruciating heartbeats before he pressed the wide door open in a noiseless arc. "After you," he said, gesturing her forward with a palm.

She stepped over the threshold and into the dimly lit foyer. Checkered black-and-white marble, polished to a gleaming sheen, stretched before them. Dual staircases, curving in graceful arcs toward the second floor, spiraled around the giant chandelier the family had ordered from France a century ago. She saw the opulent display through Ethan's eyes, seeing her home not as the employee he'd once been, but as a wildly successful man no longer impressed by the trappings of wealth.

"Father's study and the papers are this way," she said, striding down the north hall and flipping lights on in her wake. Maybe, if she maintained a businesslike professionalism, she could pretend the awful silence in the car had never happened. Maybe, with luck, he'd simply collect the island paperwork and she could survive the night unscathed.

Ethan followed at a more leisurely pace, his hands clasped behind his back as he surveyed the crown molding and artwork decorating the silk-paneled walls.

Several feet before Cate reached her father's study, the door at the far end of the hall opened. Mrs. Bartholomew bustled in from the servant wing, her graying braid draped over one shoulder and her pink housecoat wrapped around her ample girth. "Is that you, Cate?"

Cate rushed forward to clasp her aging nanny-turned-housekeeper's arthritic hands and lowered her voice to an earnest scolding. "Why aren't you in bed?"

"Oh, you know me," she replied with a reassuring pat on Cate's knuckles. "I can't sleep properly when you're off in the city."

Cate's smile felt more like an awkward grimace as she tried to usher Mrs. Bartholomew back toward her room. "Well, I'm home now, safe and sound. You can go back to bed." She pressed against the housekeeper's soft back and curved shoulder. "Go, before I feel any guiltier for ruining your night's sleep."

A sound stalled their footsteps and Mrs. Bartholomew turned to gaze down the hallway. Tipping sideways, her eyes narrowed as she squinted toward Ethan. "Who's that with you, dear?"

Cate closed her eyes and exhaled through her nose, scrambling for a lie that would appease her self-appointed mother hen without making things worse. "Nobody. It's just someone from the auction."

"Oh, my heavenly stars, I don't believe it," the housekeeper breathed. Mrs. Bartholomew abandoned Cate and raced to intersect Ethan, her slippers slapping noisily against the marble. "Ethan Hardesty, is that you?"

"Mrs. Bartholomew?" The cynical mask he'd worn all night slipped to reveal unabashed pleasure as he opened his arms and hauled the housekeeper into a hug. She squealed like a girl when he lifted her from the floor and spun her in a joyous circle before returning her back to her feet. "I can't believe you still work here!"

She gripped his hand with both of hers, her happiness at seeing him bowing her cheeks high. "Where else would I be, you big galoot?"

Cate sidled closer while they grinned at each other, hoping Mrs. Bartholomew didn't say anything incriminating.

Ethan reached to cup Mrs. Bartholomew's rounded jaw.

"You're retiring from this job," he told her. "Tonight. I won't hear of you working another day."

She tugged free of his touch, her booming laughter echoing in the cavernous hall. "You always were too bossy for your own good."

"I'm serious." He reached for her shoulders. "I just bought Cate's island for Dad and I know he'd love to have you there with him. You and he could be a couple of retirees, soaking up the island sun just like old times."

"Without you kids?" She slapped his hands aside. "Don't be ridiculous. I'm perfectly happy here and Cate still needs me." Mrs. Bartholomew reached for Cate's wrist and tugged. "Isn't that right, dear?"

Ethan's gaze narrowed on Cate as he waited for her reply, as if daring her to exploit his treasured childhood friend any more than she already had.

Cate weighed her words carefully. "You know I love having you here, but all I really need is for you to be happy," she said. "I'm grown up now, so if you're ready to retire, you'd have both my blessing and your well-deserved pension."

"Nonsense. You won't be grown up until you have a decent man in your life." She turned to Ethan as if he were her confidante and a necessary companion in getting Cate raised right. "This girl needs someone who can take care of her, no matter what she says."

"I do not!" she protested. Humiliation fired Cate's skin when she caught sight of Ethan's amused expression, and she wished the marble floor would simply open beneath her feet so she could sink out of view.

But it wasn't to be.

Instead, things got immeasurably worse.

The housekeeper's grip tightened about Cate's wrist, betraying the flash of inspiration that led Mrs. Bartholomew to snag Ethan's hand, as well. "Ethan, Cate's still as pretty as when you were a boy, isn't she?" she asked.

"Mrs. Bartholomew!" gasped Cate.

"If you agree to consider taking care of Cate for me, then maybe I will retire."

"Promise?" Ethan teased. His gaze slid to Cate's. "Because nothing would please me more than taking care of Cate."

Mrs. Bartholomew didn't appear to notice the note of sarcasm beneath his words, because she drew both Cate and Ethan's hands together before chirping, "I always knew you'd come back for her!" She patted their stacked hands and then lowered her voice to a conspiratorial tone as she leaned toward Ethan. "I'll just leave you two to sort out the details, and if you're still here at breakfast time, I'll make those cranberry waffles you love so much."

Cate yanked her hand from his the minute Mrs. Bartholomew turned. Anxious to escape her own reaction to his nearness and the horrible, awful way she wanted to crawl into a hole and die, Cate ducked around Ethan to stride back toward her father's study. She pressed her hands against her stomach, trying to stem the tide of embarrassment cinching her belly tight. Her skin burned. Her head hurt. And she wanted the night to be over. Now.

She told herself it was because she was exhausted. The stress of preparing for the auction, skipping dinner, selling the island, resurrecting a past she'd hoped to keep buried, it had all taken its toll. It had nothing to do with the way her pathetic heart had responded to the prospect of Ethan taking care of her. To the prospect of Ethan caring *for* her.

She'd agreed to bring Ethan here for one purpose, and the sooner they finished their business, the sooner she could resume her life. She didn't want Ethan to think she needed anything from him beyond the auction bid he'd promised. She was no longer an eighteen-year-old girl hopelessly in love with the caretaker's son. Craving more than he'd ever want to give just made her feel pathetic and desperate.

She didn't do desperate. Not anymore.

It wasn't until she'd reached the imposing double doors of her father's study that she heard Ethan's footsteps resume.

Cate immediately grappled with the door handle, wanting to maintain the distance between them. But his long legs had him catching up to her before her fumbling fingers could wrestle the door open. He reached for her wrist, his deep voice rippling the air beside her cheek. "I'm not going to bite you, Cate."

She jerked away from his touch and glared up at him. "I can't believe you said that to her."

"I was just making an old woman smile."

"Yeah, well, you can't get her hopes up like that when nothing's going to come of it."

He reached to cup the side of her face, skimming his thumb along her jaw as his lips curved in an enticing smile. "Who says nothing will?"

She reared back, breaking the contact. "Ethan!"

"What?"

"Please don't make things worse. I'm embarrassed enough."

"Why?"

A stupid, stupid film of tears gathered in her eyes and she blinked furiously to keep them at bay. She hadn't cried for nine years, and she wasn't about to start now. "I don't know, Ethan. Maybe because of how you've been reacting, all seductive and detached and angry and…grateful. I can't read you anymore, and it puts me at a disadvantage. I don't like it."

His expression sobered and his gaze searched hers. "I grew up, Cate, just like you did. You can't expect things to be the same."

She pressed her fingers to her temple and winced. "I know."

"So what do you say we move forward from here?" He collected her hand and then tipped her chin until she met his eyes. "Who knows where things might lead?"

Dropping her gaze, she pulled her hand free and lifted it between them. "No. Too much has happened."

"Like what?" he asked, the timbre of his voice sensitizing her nerve endings while his thumb grazed her bottom lip.

She stepped sideways, shaking her head. "Tonight is about the island paperwork. That's the only reason you're here."

His blue eyes slipped to half-mast. "No, it isn't."

"It is for me." She firmed her jaw, ignoring the tremor of awareness humming in her veins. "I don't want anything else."

"Liar."

She exhaled noisily. "Look. It's been a really long day and I can't do this right now. I just want to go to bed."

Heat flared behind his eyes. "That could be arranged."

Cate ground her teeth, berating herself for making such an artless statement. "That's not what I meant and you know it."

"Sorry, Catydid, but you can't expect me to let that Freudian slip pass," he said with abominable arrogance. "You want me. I want you. Let's do something about it."

She clamped her mouth closed and dragged in a calming breath before trusting herself to speak again. "I don't want you for anything other than friendship, Ethan. And if you keep pushing, I won't even want that."

"Your kiss said otherwise."

"It wasn't my kiss. It was *yours*," she protested.

The heat in his eyes deepened, its licking flame devouring her common sense. "It sure felt mutual to me."

Desperation sharpened her tone. "You know what, Ethan? We're done. You can see yourself out and I'll send the papers to your lawyers tomorrow." She tried to step past him, but he moved left, blocking her escape.

"You don't want my twenty-five million?"

"If this is the condition? No," she said, shoving hard against his chest. He didn't budge, and she felt as if she'd just pitted her strength against a concrete wall. Agitated and unable to do anything about it, she dropped her hands and her chin, trying to create some distance between them. "Move."

"There's no shame in wanting to finish what we started."

"No."

He tipped her chin up, refusing to grant her a retreat. "Admit you want me," he told her, the rasp of his finger against her skin sending sparks of sensation all the way to her toes. "Just a little bit."

She forced a glare to her eyes, praying he'd see the anger and not the desire that battled within. "Why don't you go ask one of your models instead? I'm sure they'd be happy to assuage the demands of your ego."

"I know," he said while a predatory light flashed in his eyes. "But where's the challenge in that?"

For a moment, Cate was rendered speechless. The fact that he was so horrifically confident in his ability to seduce any female he wished, coupled with the very real possibility that he didn't overestimate his skills at all, served to tip her mood in anger's favor. "You're no better than a stray dog, sniffing after every female who crosses your path."

In one smooth motion he closed the space between them, crowding her until she had to arch her head backward to maintain eye contact. Slowly, he bent over her and inhaled. Deeply. "Jealous?" he whispered.

"Of course not," she said, grappling for control. "They can have you with my blessing."

Ethan dipped his head, looming over her until she could see the hint of black whiskers shadowing his jaw, a masculine edginess that enhanced his dangerous appeal. His mouth, quirked with sardonic command, held a trace of threat, a hint of dark intensity that dared her to answer him truthfully. "You don't mean that, Catydid."

Cate's mood flipped right back into desire, her heart thudding heavily against her ribs. She pressed against the door, her shoulders and buttocks flattened against its substantial weight in an effort to reclaim her emotional equilibrium. It didn't help. They stood immobile for several heartbeats, their bodies nearly touching while erotic urgency hummed its way along Cate's nerves and created a knot of longing deep in her belly.

A sudden urge to surprise him, to gain the upper hand, swept through her. She wanted to eradicate his calm control, to flick her tongue against the corners of his mouth and graze her teeth along his flesh until *he* stumbled back, unnerved. She wanted him on the defensive, as subject to his own body's cravings as she.

"Besides," he crooned in a soothing, patronizing voice. "You know I don't want any of those other women." With that, he moved closer, his solid weight pressing her against the door and rendering escape impossible. His palms braced beside her head, creating a cage of muscle and sinew and bone. "I only want you."

CHAPTER SIX

CATE gasped as his thickly muscled chest wedged tight against hers. Silent and unbearably, achingly close, his breath caressed her cheek. For long, excruciating moments, he didn't speak, as if granting her body the time it needed to assimilate the weight of his.

"I want to taste you again," he finally breathed.

As insane as the impulse was, she wanted to plunge headlong into the abyss that was Ethan. She wanted to take that clever, teasing tongue of his into her mouth until he came unmoored, to scrape her fingernails over the snowy white pleats of his tuxedo shirt and feel every inch of his warm, satiny skin. "I can't," she said in a hoarse voice, thick with desire. "Please let me go."

"Ah, Catydid…" His voice seduced her, brushing even closer as if he hadn't heard her plea at all. "I don't think I can just yet."

Sensation rippled through her, pinned as she was between the cold, hard door and the hot, hard male before her. His body, so big and thick and strong, was not that of the slim boy she remembered. No longer narrow and wiry, he carried the width and breadth of a full-blooded man well into his prime. Powerful, ruthless and accustomed to claiming whatever he wanted, Ethan possessed a body to match his personality.

Determined to wrest control of the situation, or at least to balance the scales in her favor, Cate reached blindly for the door handle and wrenched it down. The latch gave way and, beneath their combined weight, the door swung inward. She stumbled backward, flailing for balance until Ethan's hands caught her upper arms and hauled her upright.

For one breathless moment, they remained unmoving, before Ethan's mouth firmed and he stepped fully into the office. He kicked the door shut behind them, plunging them into the shadowed, predawn darkness of her father's office. She gasped, her senses heightened by the absence of light. She heard his breath, as fractured as hers, as he spun her back against the closed door. And then his weight was against her again, his warm hands dragging from her shoulders to hips.

The heat of his breath against her cheek and the possessive demand of his wide palms as they mapped her curves elicited a visceral jolt of sensation deep within. She pushed against him, her resistance losing strength as her fingers met the hard contours of his chest. She absorbed the swell of thick muscle, the sturdy ladder of rib, then stiffened when his insistent exploration of her body detoured to the sensitive underside of her breast.

"Don't fight me," he rasped.

She bit her lip, failing miserably in her attempt to keep from becoming lost in the fragrance of him, the salty, musky, sex-scented incense that made her heart beat in heavy, painful blows against her chest. "Why are you doing this to me?" she asked in a tortured whisper.

"You know why," he muttered. "I've never stopped wanting you, never stopped wondering how it could be between us."

Yes. She no longer wished to fight him. Intellectually, she realized Ethan was a danger to her. He threatened the calm serenity of her life in a way that both frightened and worried her. Yet somehow, she couldn't force herself to send him away.

Not yet. It had been so long since she'd felt this way. So long since she'd wanted to be touched.

But she didn't want to make the wrong decision, take the crazy risk, and lose her heart in the process. Because no matter what lies she told herself, she knew if she allowed herself to love him again, to open her heart and soul when he felt nothing for her, the pain would drive her to her knees.

You've endured the pain already, a small voice reminded her. *Why not enjoy the pleasure for just one night?*

Yes. Her body ached to know his. In truth, it had never stopped yearning for the touch of his hand, the silky slide of his mouth. Her skin, her breasts, her innermost core, craved him. Her body begged her to indulge in just one stolen interlude of pleasure here in the shadows, where secrets could remain hidden and scars could remain unseen. Just once, she wanted to tip from the precarious ledge of arousal into shuddering fulfillment.

Just once. With him.

She'd waited so long.

"Just let me—" He broke off as her fingers rose to trace the harsh ridge of his jaw, the bristly contours of his chin. Frozen beneath her touch, his agitated breath buffeted the tips of her fingers as she gingerly brushed his parted lips.

Reveling in her ability to distract him and relishing the exquisite rush of arousal, Cate drew out the anticipation, slowly running her fingers along the lean lines of his face, up to his brow and the cool strands of his thick, wavy hair. She reacquainted herself with the shape of his skull, the curve of his nape, the resilient strength of his neck.

It felt like a homecoming, for whether she wished it or not, her body remembered his with undeniable clarity. She wanted to chart every inch of his skin, to test her memory against the changes that time had wrought. She wanted to taste him, lick the salt from his flesh and bury her nose in the scented cove at

the base of his throat. Heated lust, thick and humid and voracious, poured off her in dizzying waves, urging her to forget
all the reasons that being with Ethan was so dangerous.

She sucked in a breath and dropped her hands back to his
shoulders, imagining the sleek cords of muscle and satiny skin
beneath the formal layers of cotton and wool. Wild, reckless
and consumed by her own risky daring, she allowed her hands
to glide to his back and then lower, lower and lower still, until
with a subtle twist of wrist, her fingertips pressed delicately
against the curve of his buttocks. He responded immediately,
grinding his groin against hers and shoving her bodily against
the door.

Excitement tore through her, her nerves tingling at the
press of his hot, tensile length against her concealed flesh.
Memories of his swollen hardness against her belly, of his
mouth against her breasts, had her virginal flesh swelling
with wet, aching, frustrated need.

"Ethan..." she murmured on a pleading moan.

His breath escaped on a hiss and then his hands dropped
to her shoulders. He lowered his head, his mouth brushing
her eyelids, her cheeks and her lips with a softness borne of
exquisite control. His ability to sip when she wanted him to
devour frustrated her, and she squirmed to get closer.

Ever in control, he skirted her advances, his mouth coast-
ing from one side of her jaw to the other. He tarried for just a
moment at her mouth, then continued his exploration down her
neck and back up to the sensitive lobe of her ear. Blindly, she
turned to catch his mouth, craving the full pressure of his lips
against hers. He relented, slowly, claiming her by agonizing
increments and eliciting a raw whimper of pleasure when he
finally sank his mouth fully against hers.

Limp with relief, Cate opened to him, welcoming the questing demands of his tongue. He tasted her aggressively, probing
her mouth with a poignant, practiced skill that eradicated her

ability to think, let alone resist. The tempo of her breath turned frantic, while inner muscles tensed with delicious need. She wanted to climb his hips, to straddle him in an embrace so consuming, so deep, that his flesh became indiscernible from hers.

Heedless of the fragile tightrope of arousal she danced upon, Cate rocked against him, seeking the intimate rhythm she'd craved for as long as she'd been a woman. The thought of having him deep inside her, filling her until she could take no more, sent a rush of liquid heat between her legs and toppled her into mindless desire.

Lifting her high upon his thigh, Ethan rounded his shoulders over hers and hauled her closer. With one hand clamped under her buttocks and the other reaching low to hook behind her knee, he spread her thighs and ground the ridge of his arousal against her aching center. Back, forth, then back again, he slowly increased the pace until their labored breathing mingled into muted sounds of primal mating.

Cate moaned and squirmed, kissing him in a feverish frenzy. He returned each kiss, as if relearning all the ways their lips could fit together, his breathy groans of approval firing her need to have him deep, deep inside her. Finally. Oh, finally.

She arched against him, trying to relieve the knotted pressure in her breasts. Her tight, puckered nipples abraded his chest through her lace bra and silk dress, drawing a low growl from deep in his throat.

"Take me upstairs…" He feasted on her mouth while his fingers lifted to her breast, plucking its erect tip through silken layers. "Take me to your bed," he breathed into her mouth.

In bed, with both of them naked, he'd see her scars. He'd see the ravages of the accident and the multiple surgeries that had saved her life. He'd either pity her or leave her, and she could bear neither. So she reached between their fused bellies, searching for his erect length. "No," she said, pressing her palm against him as she rocked with need. "I want you now. Here."

"Here." His hand caught hers, stalling her exploration while his breath beat against her forehead.

"Yes." She twisted her hand from his and dipped lower, curving her fingers around the thick base of his arousal. A fiery jolt of sensation accompanied her exploration, but she didn't waver in her purpose, her fingers trailing over the contours of his erection.

Ethan stiffened, his efforts to remain still sending a trembling quake of reaction through his limbs.

"Cate," he gasped as she worked the top button free and gingerly lowered the zipper. Hungrily, she reached for him, sliding her palm beneath the elastic band of his underwear. They both sucked in a shuddering inhale as she freed him from the constricting confines of skin-warmed cotton and heated wool. Trembling with excitement, Cate curled a hot grip around his thick circumference and delicately squeezed.

Growling low in his throat, Ethan surged forward, crushing her hand between them. He kissed her, his tongue delving deep while he slowly dragged her hands out to the side.

"Don't rush," he whispered while he bunched her skirt high enough to reveal her panties to his questing fingers. He dragged his fingers over her thighs, crouching as he slid her underwear down to her trembling ankles. His breath, hot and damp, warmed her bared stomach as he bent close to her groin. He lifted first one foot, then the other, until she was naked beneath her skirt.

Once she stood barefoot before him, she reached for him, trying to draw him back up. He succumbed to her nonverbal plea, slowly standing as her breath rent the air in choppy waves. She felt his hands slowly shifting her dress back up, bunching the delicate fabric as his hands glided over her bare skin. When he reached her waist again, he pressed her against the door, trapping the fabric between her back and the cool panel of wood.

With one hand curved over the notch of her waist, he dipped his knees and charted her bare hip and abdomen with the other wide, warm palm. She gasped when a twist of his wrist had his hot fingers cupping the damp juncture of her thighs. Heat flooded her chest and she reached to regain a bit of control. Undeterred, he snagged her hands and pressed them flat against the door at her back. She felt her core grow distressingly damp and she squirmed, trying to free her hands. "Ethan," she panted. "Hurry."

"Shh," he breathed. "If you insist on doing this against a door, I'm damn well going to take my time. So stop trying to drive the train and just enjoy the ride, Catydid."

Swallowing against a rush of nervousness, she waited obediently as he returned his hand to her inner thigh. Curling his fingers until his knuckles grazed the transition from flesh to curls, he wandered idly over the triangular thatch of heat. She sucked in a breath and tipped toward his fingers, her hands itching to guide his. But she forced herself to wait, savoring the blinding rise of excitement.

After several slow, meandering circles, he paused for a moment, then ventured lower, brushing a delicate whisper of sensation over her flesh. She jumped a little and he removed his touch, only to expertly slide both his palms down her quivering outer thighs. She whimpered at the delay and she heard his masculine huff of laughter before he leisurely detoured back up. Using one wide palm to part her legs, he returned the fingers of his other hand to the apex of her thighs. Cate felt a jolt of primal pleasure beneath his touch, at having the passions of this beautiful man focused solely on her.

His fingers skimmed her with aching tenderness. Her hands twitched helplessly against the door and she inhaled sharply when his fingertip danced delicately over the entrance to her body, teasing at the yielding threshold of her virginity until aching pleas of incoherent encouragement rose in her throat.

Reaching behind her, Ethan banded his arm beneath her buttocks and hauled her close. His mouth dipped to hers and soon, his kiss turned voracious, primitive and demanding, creating a blinding contrast to the tender, leisurely exploration of his gentle fingers. Bombarded with sensations too splintered to categorize, she closed her eyes on a ragged gasp and dug her nails into the door at her back.

He tormented her with wet, circling nudges, grazing and skimming and delicately exploring until she drove down against his hand with tight, clamping eagerness. Her flesh throbbed. Ached. She writhed against his palm, suspended above a chasm of release so acute she couldn't breathe. Then he hurtled her over the edge and wrenching pleasure closed over her, obliterating thought and drowning her in great, shuddering waves of sensation.

She gasped for air, spasms rocketing through her abdomen and legs, sending a riptide of ecstasy down her limbs. After endless moments of suspended, elongated rapture, her orgasm eased into subtle ripples of satisfied completion, and a plaintive whimper escaped her lips.

Ethan gave her a final kiss, then dipped to a kneel, his hands splaying over the still-quivering cove of her stomach. The rough satin of his tongue dragged along her inner thigh, then strayed higher. Her head lolled weakly against the door and she moved a languid hand to stall further progress. "Ethan," she said, embarrassed heat rioting through her as he knelt to inhale her musk. "Don't…" But it was too late. His lips were already on her.

Violent trembles overtook her, and she struggled to stay upright. Shaking, she reached for his head, threading her fingers blindly through slippery strands of black silk. "Ethan," she rasped, unable to think anything beyond his name.

His mouth sucked at her, the feathery wetness of his tongue drawing moans from her throat. She couldn't think, couldn't move, and her gasping breaths served as mindless punctuation to his silent seduction. Pleasure coiled high once more, the tension climbing in waves with every pull of his mouth.

"I can't," she panted, her hands twisting in his hair. "Ethan...oh, Ethan, please..."

He took pity on her desperate plea and surged to his feet. She heard the telltale snick of a condom being ripped open, felt him withdraw for the barest lapse of time as he expertly slid the lubricated latex down over his jutting length. Before she had a chance to reach for him, he'd lifted her within his arms again. One arm banded tightly about her ribs while the other wrapped beneath her buttocks. She was trapped against him, spread to his will and open to his desires.

Ethan bent to kiss her, his heated breath wafting over her lips. She felt the thick pressure of his erection, the head of his penis pushing against her vulnerable core.

The feel of her closing around him, hot and unbearably tight, seemed to drive Ethan's urgency even higher. He surged upward while his hands against her hips drove her weight down. A fractured gasp tore from Cate's throat as the vulnerable tissues of her body rent to accommodate his inexorable invasion. He was deep inside her and Cate tensed in pain, her fingernails digging sharply into his shoulders.

Ethan froze, the evidence of her body's resistance finally registering beneath the thick fog of lust. He reared back in astonishment. "Tell me you're not a virgin," he breathed.

"I'm not a virgin," she lied, even as residual pain hitched within her voice. To hide her reaction, she leaned forward to kiss his lips, hoping he didn't detect the wince that tightened her mouth.

"Cate." His hand rose to grip her jaw and he pressed her back, his breath buffeting her in the darkness.

"It doesn't matter," she said, reaching to draw him into her arms again. "It's all right. Just don't stop." She clamped him to her chest with such desperation, she couldn't draw a breath. He was part of her now, and she couldn't release him. Not yet. So she reclaimed him with everything at her disposal, drawing him in with a deep, rhythmic pull of her inner muscles and a tight, secure squeeze of her arms.

His resistance weakened and then, with a shuddering exhalation, he leaned to kiss her fiercely. For several long moments he kept his body still while his tongue stroked her. When she began to squirm within his arms, he began to thrust again in a slow, gentle rhythm. The tight sting of his assault relented a bit, though Cate no longer cared.

All she wanted right now was to possess Ethan, to contain his hard arousal, and to stay with him through this essential act they'd been moving toward for their entire lives.

Hissing strained breath through clenched teeth, Ethan braced his legs and pumped hard, driving deeper, pummeling the inner recesses of her body as he climbed toward release. A triumphant grunt of pleasure filled the air as he stiffened within her. His climax, hard, fierce and primal, seemed to last forever. Cate clung to his still-clothed body, dragging her open lips over his panting mouth, his whiskered chin and the salt-streaked column of his neck.

Ethan shuddered and bowed over her, holding her close for a long, endless time. Slowly, the tension in his muscles eased and he returned her to stand against the door. Her inner muscles twinged in protest and she gingerly lowered her arms to her waist as her skirt slid back down to her knees. She felt Ethan's gaze on her silhouette, and dipped to collect her discarded underwear and shoes. She didn't want to deal with his questions yet. Not yet. She didn't want to think about the future. Or the past. She just wanted to burrow against his chest, curl up against his big, warm body and save their regrets for after he'd held her for a while.

But he'd already withdrawn from her, returning his clothes to order and retreating to pace tight, tense circles in the waning darkness. She watched his agitated shadow in aching silence, pressed the wad of silk and shoes against her quivering stomach, and tried not to think. Beneath the cold distance wicking the heat that had gathered between them, she felt his simmering fury begin to boil.

"Cate," she heard him say, and his voice was low and ominous. "Why the hell didn't you tell me you were a virgin?"

She closed her eyes and dropped her head, staring through the shadows at her bare feet. "I didn't think it was important," she mumbled.

"Not important." He strode to the wall of windows overlooking the beach and shoved the drapes aside with a violent, angry jerk. Dawn's light refracted off the water, casting a nimbus of apricot and gold about Ethan's imposing frame. He pressed a knotted fist against the glass and inhaled twice before turning back to face her. "In what universe is giving a man your virginity not important?"

When she averted her eyes, he strode back to confront her.

He gripped her jaw with tensile fingers and tipped her head back, forcing her to meet his dangerous gaze. "If you attach so little importance to the deed, how is it you've lasted ten years without some other man finding his way between your thighs?"

She lifted one shoulder and angled a glance beyond his furious features. "Other men desire my money, not me. I wanted to be desired for more than my benefit to their bottom line."

"Sleeping with a man doesn't mean you have to fund his future portfolios."

"I didn't say it does," she protested. "But it *is* about mutual respect, and attraction, and—"

"Then why the hell did you allow *me* to take your virginity?" he exploded, releasing her as if he'd touched flame and then shoving his hands through his hair. "Good God, Cate, what were you thinking?"

Cate grappled for a suitable lie. "I don't know. Maybe it's like you said. I wanted you. You wanted me. We had unfinished business."

"Unfinished business?" He was back, gripping her shoulders while his eyes flashed. "And you think this takes care of it?" he asked with a bark of incredulous laughter. "Let me be perfectly clear, Cate Carrington. Fifteen minutes between your virginal thighs doesn't even begin to scratch the surface."

A frisson of alarm went through her chest, turning her skin cold. "Well, fifteen minutes is all you get, Ethan. I won't allow this to happen again."

"The hell you won't," he ground out before hauling her to her toes and crushing her to his chest again. "You'll give me everything I want, whenever and however I want it." And then he was kissing her again, mercilessly, plying her mouth with a mastery that bespoke of domination, rather than pleasure. And though she knew it was madness to respond, to grant him any ownership of her will, Cate couldn't keep herself from surrendering.

She didn't have the strength to fight him, to resist the compelling draw of his mouth and hands. Before long, her shoes had again tumbled to the floor and she stood melting within his arms, succumbing to his kisses with a feverish moan.

Only after her weakness was apparent to both of them did Ethan step back. His choppy breath stirred the small hairs along her forehead as he spoke. "We're not finished until *I* say we're finished. Understood?"

"No!" Cate wrenched free of him. "We're finished now!"

She turned her back and jerked open the door, conscious of her aching muscles, of the damp stickiness between her thighs.

Terrified that he'd convince her to stay, Cate catapulted back out into the hall, blindly running from the evidence of her bad judgment. Before she'd even realized her destination, she'd escaped through a side door and bolted barefoot past the empty barn and corral, past the dismantled jumping course and arena, to the sloped beach that held too many memories of the past. Of the time before pain. Before either of them had hurt the other.

She stumbled, falling to her bare knees in the rough sand. The threat of tears burned her eyes and she rocked forward, wrapping her arms around her ribs as she relived the past few humiliating moments with Ethan. She should have seen it coming, should have heeded the warning her mind had been screaming since she'd first seen him.

She'd been so eager to feel something besides pain and doubt and guilt that she'd ignored what her heart already knew, what she'd recognized when they danced. So she had no one else to blame but herself. Not really. She'd earned his hatred, understood his need for revenge.

But then, how did he expect to gain it? Did he wish to strip her of her pride? Her virginity? He'd managed to do both within the space of a few hours. What else could he demand before he'd be finished with her? What more could he want, when she had nothing left to give?

The only thing she was good at anymore was surviving. Coping. Hadn't she learned that lesson time and time again? Hadn't she rejected the only man she'd ever loved, then sustained injuries so severe that she'd never lead a normal life again? Never be a real woman? A wife? A mother?

She clenched her hands into fists against her quaking rib cage, trying to corral the pain as her throat tightened and burned. Bereft and hurting, she swallowed fiercely, holding back the tears she refused to shed. As much as she wanted peace, as much as she wanted forgiveness, she'd never receive it no matter how eloquent her request. Not after what she'd done.

Ethan hated her. She knew it as surely as she knew her own scars. Apologizing to him and giving him her virginity didn't change a thing.

She'd been a fool to think it could.

CHAPTER SEVEN

ETHAN stood alone in the empty office feeling disoriented, bruised and strangely adrift. Never, not in his wildest imaginings, had he considered this night unfolding the way that it had. He'd envisioned himself in complete control of the situation, his emotions and Cate's responses.

The years he'd spent away from her had brought sexual experience and expertise he'd grown to rely upon. He knew how to seduce a woman, how to gauge her reactions and arousal. He knew how to orchestrate a woman's responses down to each shuddering sigh and had exercised the finely honed skill too many times to count. This was the first time he'd lost the distance he always maintained, the first time he'd nearly lost himself in his own practiced art of seduction.

An unwelcome sense of dissatisfaction, of frustrated anger and resentment, rioted within his veins. By failing to meet his expectations, Cate had upended everything. She had turned the tables on him. Made him lose control.

Ethan Hardesty did not lose control.

Nor did he bear the brunt of female rejection. Not anymore.

Furious with his own weakness, he dragged a palm over his mouth. The faint aroma of Cate clung to his fingers, resurrecting memories of her responsive skin and widespread thighs.

His lungs tightened and he felt the stirrings of lust yet

again. He relived the moments when he'd moved deep inside her, the tight flesh surrounding him until he thought he'd go mad with his release. Her low, breathy moans.

He wanted her again.

He wanted to taste her mouth, lick her skin and bury himself so deep inside he forgot where he ended and she began.

God damn it. No, God damn *her*. Why the hell did she have to be a virgin? He understood why she'd been untouched ten years ago, when they were both so young. He'd respected her desire to wait for marriage, had gritted his teeth and taken multiple cold swims in the ocean because of it. But to wait another ten years?

Why had she allowed *him* to claim her virginity, instead of one of the countless others who'd queued up for the opportunity? And why did she *still* arouse the feelings he thought he'd eradicated forever ago? He didn't want the confusion, the suspicion and the inconvenient desire to please her. And he sure as hell didn't want to lust after her with an intensity he'd felt only for her. Only her.

And yet his irrational mind, his body and his wretched, cursed soul, didn't seem to care. He wanted her despite the lies. He wanted her despite the past and the anger he felt toward her. No matter how many years had elapsed, no matter how many other women he'd seduced, he still wanted her.

He lifted the heels of his hands to his eyes and pressed. Hard. Trying to will away his obsession and his lack of control. She was not the Cate he'd once loved. That Cate didn't exist anywhere outside of his feverish adolescent fantasies. She never had. He knew it.

She'd claimed to want him to be happy and successful, when in reality, she'd never even thought of him as a man capable of taking care of himself. And then she'd claimed to have grieved his absence. That she'd felt guilty for her lies.

As if that made any difference at all.

He dropped his hands, firming his jaw and embracing the fresh surge of resolve that thickened his blood. He wasn't done with her, no matter what she claimed. She could run away, she could say no, but they weren't finished until he said they were.

He'd barely made it back to his offices in New York when Ethan opened his door to greet the private messenger Cate had already dispatched. Looking at the prim rectangular envelope, embossed with the Carrington crest, he felt a flare of anger so acute, his chest went tight with it.

She thought to complete their business via a messenger?

"Shall I wait for a reply?" the delivery boy asked.

"No," Ethan barked. He tossed a fifty at the kid and then slammed the door in his smiling face.

A scant two minutes later, with Cate's papers strewn out upon his desk, the pen he held snapped in two. Rage surged anew as he stared at her tidy little signature at the bottom of the page.

She'd signed before he'd transferred a single cent of the twenty-five million he'd agreed to pay. As if she thought she'd get rid of him so easily, stamped and sealed and dispensed with like so much inconvenient rubbish.

Just like before. Only this time, he wasn't playing her game.

This time, she would pay.

And he'd be glad.

Forty-eight hours later, he interrupted his broker's protest. "I don't care about the cost. Buy them. I want the controlling shares, and I want them yesterday," he said before slamming his phone down with an audible slap.

He scanned the faxed transaction report another stock-broker had just sent over from his Tokyo office. The realization that everything was falling into place exactly as he wished coiled deep in his gut, tantalizing him with the promise of justice, of the painful retribution Cate so richly deserved.

Within the hour, he'd own fifty-two percent of Carrington Industries. A majority holding. After two whirlwind days of purchasing the publicly traded shares under a series of different names, utilizing multiple subsidiary businesses beneath the umbrella of his parent company to broker the transactions, the controlling interest in Cate's company belonged to him. Ethan Hardesty.

He didn't waste time examining how his emotions seemed to waver unpredictably between triumph and doubt. He didn't allow himself to entertain any second thoughts.

Cate deserved whatever punishment he meted out.

By eight o'clock that night, he arrived at Studio 9 in downtown Manhattan, ready to implement the next step of his plan. The white penthouse loft was equipped with scores of ghouls, ghosts and glow-in-the-dark skeletons. Discordant music wailed in the background and dry ice smoke billowed from punch fountains set up in the corners. It took him precious minutes just to wend his way through pumpkins, hay bales and stalks of dried corn to reach the crowded rooftop venue.

By the time he located Cate, his frustration had neared its peak. She stood in a knot of slavering men, her costume that of a very elegant, subdued Cinderella. Fit to perfection, the blue-and-silver velvet gown hugged her curves and displayed her long, lean body to advantage.

She'd wrapped her pale gold hair into a twisted knot atop her head, and shiny strands of it had slipped free to caress her pinkened cheek and fragile jaw. With her haunting beauty and long, white gloves, she looked enough like a fabled princess to make any man believe in fairy tales.

Unfortunately, the desire flooding Ethan was very much grounded in reality.

He wanted to cup that heart-shaped face, run his thumb

over those rosy lips, and kiss the tip of her chilled nose before dipping lower to plunder her fully. The urge to steal her away to someplace private and warm brought a heaviness to his groin and drove him toward her with renewed resolve.

As he walked toward her, she lifted an arm and smiled. Soft and genuine, her smile snagged at a part of his soul he'd thought ruthlessly buried. It took three seconds, his heart rising within his chest, before he realized her smile wasn't for him.

No, it was for the idiotic interloper who now blocked his view, worming his way through the crowd with two steaming mugs in his hands. The man reached her, pressed one mug into her hand, then moved to stand close, as if exerting a proprietary claim before anyone else could snatch her away. From the look on the man's face, he was besotted.

Ethan was in no mood to tolerate another corps of Cate's admirers tonight. He'd bitten back the urge to bare his teeth and snap at them like an enraged bear while they circled her at the Carrington auction. But the urge was back twice as strong now. She belonged to *him*. He'd paid for her with his soul, and until he was done with her, he was not disposed to share.

Once Ethan reached the periphery of her group, he caught Cate's eye. Her hands jerked, sloshing scalding liquid over the rim of her mug and onto the weasel simpering at her side. She blushed furiously and then blurted a distressed apology, leaning to brush at the man's dampened forearm. Her lackey had dressed as a prisoner, complete with striped pajamas and a length of chain with its requisite ball.

Ethan moved closer, then reached for her mug. He handed it off to the man plucking at his wet sleeve and then wrapped a hand around Cate's elbow. "Sorry, but Cate and I have some business to attend to." He looked down at the blustering peacock at her side and offered a challenging smile. "You don't mind, do you?"

The man's nostrils flared while his face turned a satisfying shade of beet. "Actually, I—"

"It really can't wait," he interrupted.

"Ethan," she began, twisting within his arm, "you can't just—"

"What's that, Catydid?"

His eyes trapped hers, and this time she couldn't seem to pull her gaze away, even when her prolonged silence made the moment grow awkward. He wanted to lick the dot of whipped cream from her upper lip, taste her chilled skin and lower that enticing layer of blue velvet that clung to her breasts until he felt her smooth, pliable flesh beneath his palms.

The man at her side cleared his throat twice, breaking the spell, then blew into his curled fist. Cate stepped back with a flustered frown, rubbing her elbow with her free hand. "Ethan, I don't think—"

"Then stop thinking," he said before dragging her bodily toward the studio's interior.

CHAPTER EIGHT

CATE pulled hard against his hand while her heart rose to clamor against her throat. She wasn't ready to be alone with Ethan again. Not yet. Though her skin sang beneath his touch, she wasn't ready to relinquish her control, her judgment and her ability to think clearly. And she wasn't foolish enough to believe she could avoid any of the three.

Their night together had taught her that where Ethan was concerned, her resolve vanished as readily as the morning mist before the sun. She wasn't strong enough to resist him. "Ethan, stop it," she said, prying fruitlessly at his curled fingers. "We're being rude."

Rudeness was apparently no deterrent, as his pace didn't slow until he'd ushered her into a quiet interior corner partially concealed by a cloud of white mist and panels of orange and black crepe paper.

"You shouldn't be here," she told him, her heart filling her throat as she finally yanked free of his hold. "You weren't even invited."

He stopped and squared off in front of her, blocking her escape. "How do you know?"

She flushed, her hands clammy within her white gloves. "I checked the guest list."

His smile told her he misinterpreted the statement to his

advantage. "How gratifying to know you were hoping for my attendance."

"I wasn't!" she blurted. "I only checked to confirm that you *weren't* going to be here."

"Ah," he said with a slow nod. His glance traced her eyes, her cheeks and her mouth, warm and close and terrifying. "Then why haven't you raised an alarm or told me to leave?"

Somehow, she managed to retain a calm, social tone as she shot him an imperious glare. "Maybe I should. You have a disconcerting habit of showing up where you aren't wanted, thinking you can just monopolize my time and drag me off to various corners of your choosing."

"Would you have preferred that I come to your home and drag you off to your bed?"

"Of course not!" she gasped.

He shrugged. "Then you should be grateful that by coming here, yet another worthy cause will benefit." He tipped his chin toward the knot of New York's Who's Who clustered behind them. "That is what you're all about, isn't it? Worthy causes?"

How is it that he managed to make it sound like an insult? "I have no problem with you making a donation in support of the arts," she huffed. "It's your manhandling of *me* that is the problem."

"Really." His blue eyes glinted with a feral gleam as he performed a blatant perusal of her body. "Because I seem to remember it was *you* who manhandled *me* the last time we were together."

An incendiary blush climbed toward her hairline. "Only you would be ungentlemanly enough to bring that up."

His mouth curved into a wicked, enticing grin she'd never seen before. "Since when have I claimed to be a gentleman?"

"You couldn't be even if you wanted to," she snapped. "You don't know the first thing about it."

He encompassed the studio behind them with a dismissive flick of his thumb. "Whereas all the pantywaists behind us do?"

"At least they know how to treat a woman with respect."

"I have no doubt of that," he teased, leaning forward to breathe his question against her ear. "So tell me, Cate. How's that working out for you?"

An intoxicating rush of desire rose in her veins, and she lurched back a step, whacking her heel against the wall and nearly stumbling.

Ethan smiled as she regained her balance. "Badly, I take it?"

She scowled. "It was working just fine until you showed up."

One of his square hands moved to stroke the side of her neck, brushing the skin beneath her ear with a feathery touch. "Liar."

She shrugged off his touch. "I'm going back to the party now."

"So soon?" he asked. He stepped closer, crowding her even farther into the corner, his breath stirring the air at her forehead. "But it's so much more fun to spar with me than with that striped windbag out there, don't you think?"

She tensed while a torrent of longing winnowed through her. "Why are you doing this?" she breathed while his free fingers threaded beneath the frothy capped sleeve of her costume.

His expression sobered. "Because I don't like how we ended things."

"It doesn't matter. It's over. We're over."

Other than the light, glancing touch of his fingers against her upper arm, he didn't move. "No, Catydid. We're not."

"I thought I made myself clear." She twisted her arm from his touch, forcing firmness into her tone. "We're finished. You had your one night, and that's all I'm willing to give you. You hate me, and I'm okay with that. Maybe I even deserve it. But don't ask me to spend more time with you when I know how you feel about me."

He remained immobile, refusing to grant her the escape she so desperately wanted. Instead, he dipped his chin and studied her resolute expression. "Give me five minutes."

Tendrils of longing curled through her limbs, tempting her to listen to him. But she shook her head and met his eyes with an implacable stare. "What would be the point?"

Leaning close enough for his breath to kiss her forehead, he whispered, "It would give me the chance to convince you that we aren't finished yet."

Denial warred with desire as she arched away from his nearness. "But we are."

"We don't have to be."

A choked laugh rent her throat. "Yes, we do."

"Why?"

"Why?" She held up a gloved hand, disbelief pitching her voice high. "Don't be obtuse, Ethan. You and I both know there's too much baggage, too many hurt feelings and too many awful things that can't be unsaid."

He moved until her raised hand pressed against his warm chest. "Then we start over." He inhaled, his eyes dipping to her mouth and then returning. "We forget about the past and move forward."

Her pulse beat erratically within her ears, urging her to give him another chance, to throw caution to the wind and indulge in the passionate affair he offered, for however long it lasted. "No," she said, pulling her hand back to her waist. "The past won't disappear just because you want it to."

He nodded soberly. "You're right. But it doesn't have to sabotage our future, either."

"What future?"

"A future without regrets."

"I've lived with too many regrets already. And I'd be a fool if I allowed you to seduce me into more."

"What if you don't regret it?"

"How could I not? You haven't forgiven me, and until you do, you'll continue to react with distance, insincere gratitude and cruelty, no matter how many times we sleep together. You can't ask me to open myself up to that."

"Even if you owe it to me?"

"I owe it to you?"

Ethan answered her with silence.

"I'm sorry. But I can't accept this...this being with you without being with you." She blinked while her stomach twisted beneath her ribs. "It's too hard."

He studied her face without blinking. "I can make it easy."

"How?"

His head tipped toward hers. "Invite me to your bed, and I'll show you."

"Invite you...?" She gaped at him, her thoughts reeling. "You can't be serious."

"I am," he promised in a soft voice. "I plan to dismantle every one of your defenses. I won't quit until I succeed."

Her pulse fluttered with heated awareness. But she forced herself to remain outwardly unaffected by his outrageous words. "You're wasting your time."

He leaned close enough that his scent filled her nostrils, and quietly warned, "Maybe. Maybe not. I want you, and I always get what I want. Right now, I want you in my bed. Naked beneath me. Watching."

A wave of wanting flooded her limbs, warring with the

panic that coiled deep within her stomach. "I'm not sleeping with you again."

The challenge flared behind his eyes, then disappeared behind an inscrutable blue. "You underestimate my powers of persuasion, sweet." He leaned to brush his mouth against her ear. "Shall we test your resistance?"

Tendrils of longing curled through her limbs, tempting her to succumb yet again. But she turned her head from his, desperately grasping for equilibrium. For sanity. "No."

Taking advantage of her exposed ear, he dipped to whisper, "How about I tell you all the ways I plan to convince you otherwise?"

Fear and arousal joined the battle as she inched another step backward. "No."

"I'll start by talking about your hair," he murmured, his strong fingers and thumbs sliding along her neck toward her upswept hair. "And how I intend to drag its satiny ends over your bare skin." He reached for a loose tendril that curled over her collarbone and the backs of his knuckles brushed the ridge of her jaw. "I plan to paint your breasts with this platinum silk until you arch beneath my hand and beg for the pull of my mouth."

She wanted to refuse him, to push him away, but her limbs wouldn't cooperate. Instead, she merely stood frozen while her pulse beat erratically within her ears, deep within her womb and against a rib cage that felt ten sizes too small.

"And then I'll talk about the sweet wine of your mouth." His thumb lifted to skim the curve of her lower lip, tugging it down to caress the sensitive inner flesh. "I'd tell of how I dream of your lips, of how I take your tongue into my mouth and taste you in my sleep."

She swallowed thickly, her breath deteriorating into shallow, uneven pants.

"I want to consume you, Cate, to lick and taste and devour every glorious inch of you."

Why do you think I'm so scared?

"I want your scent on my skin." His nostrils flared and he leaned closer, his low voice lulling her into drugged compliance. "I want your mouth on me. I want to bury myself in your heat until I can think of nothing beyond the pleasure we share. I want to feel your pulse around me and know you're mine."

You've already given him your virginity, a small voice wheedled. *As long as you don't love him again, how much worse can it get?*

It can, and you know it.

Every cell screamed at her brain to be quiet, to lose herself in the terrifying, intoxicating things he did to her body. She wanted the touch of his fingers, the silky rasp of his tongue within her mouth, on her flesh. Inside her.

But that would never be enough, and she knew it. The hunger to feel his bare skin, to explore the coves and hollows of his naked body, was more than a simple, containable physical need. It was more than mere lust, and she'd be lost if she allowed herself to forget that fact.

She forced her listing eyelids to remain open and locked her knees to keep from swaying toward him. "Stop it, Ethan."

His breath heated her trembling lips, close but not touching. "I haven't even done anything, sweet."

Mustering her resolve, she forced herself to stiffen. To withdraw. "You're talking," she said, pushing against his chest until he straightened. "And I want you to stop."

He stared at her for a long, quiet moment, her fractured breath beating the air between them. "I may not seduce you tonight, but I will take my pleasure with you, Cate. And you're going to allow it because you want me as much as I want you. Our night together proved it."

The memory of what he'd done to her, of what she'd allowed

him to do, fired her neck and face with unbearable heat. "It proved nothing beyond a mutual curiosity, ten years in the making," she said.

Taking in her blush, his mouth quirked in amusement. "Right. And you're not remotely curious to see how much better it can be between us, now that you're no longer a virgin."

"My curiosity has already been satisfied, thank you very much."

"You're welcome," he quipped.

The flames of arousal licked lower, making the heavy velvet of her dress feel far too warm. "I liked you better when you weren't so cocky," she managed, hoping her flippant remark would distract him from the flushed readiness of her skin.

"With good reason," he agreed without compunction. "You had much more control of me then."

"Well, I'm not impressed with the new you," she insisted. "I far prefer a bit of give and take with a man. You know, a man who takes what I want into consideration."

"Then why are you alone?"

His blue eyes, bright in their intensity, demanded that she answer truthfully. But truth was the last thing she could afford. "Because I choose to be."

"Because no one is good enough for Cate Carrington?"

She huffed out an exasperated breath. "Don't be ridiculous."

"Tell me why, then."

"You're only interested because I haven't immediately fallen under your spell and then begged you to save me from my life of self-imposed solitude."

An arched brow met the challenge of her words.

"Look, I know you won't take me against my will, so all this posturing is getting you nowhere. I will never agree to sleep with you of my own volition. You may as well accept it now."

"Then you'd better grow accustomed to telling me no. Repeatedly."

"Don't think I won't."

"If you don't send me away in the next five seconds," he said, "I'll interpret it as tacit permission to ravage you right where we stand."

A crazy mix of emotions spiraled through her—amusement, arousal, irritation and stubborn rebellion. Ethan had never been arrogant before, but she found the intensity of his self-confidence both disturbing and attractive. If for nothing else, she hesitated the specified five seconds simply because she wanted to see just how far his bravado would carry him.

"Time's up," he breathed, moving close.

She opened her mouth to dismiss him, but he bent his head and caught her words with a kiss. He drugged her with its intensity, taking advantage of her surprise to delve deep, to suck and lick and nibble until her resistance melted like warm sap from her pliant limbs.

Only then did he draw back, his breath lifting the fine hairs at her temple. His long fingers moved to stroke the side of her neck, brushing the skin beneath her ear with a feathery touch. "Change your mind yet?"

Bemused by the teasing note in his voice, she lifted heavy lids to meet his gaze. His mouth, normally crooked in a sardonic curve, looked almost relaxed. But his eyes were anything but. She felt as if she were the prey to his predator, caught in a web of pleasure so intense, she craved capture. "You know I haven't," she finally whispered.

He dipped his head to kiss her again, until her breath hitched hard in her chest and her sense of propriety blurred. Again, he withdrew. Again, he looked at her as if he wanted

Get 2 books Free!
Plus, receive a FREE mystery gift

If you have enjoyed reading this Modern romance story, then why not take advantage of this **FREE** book offer and we'll send you two more titles from this series absolutely **FREE**!

Accepting your **FREE** books and **FREE** mystery gift places you under no obligation to buy anything.

As a member of the Mills & Boon Book Club™ you'll receive your favourite Series books up to 2 months ahead of the shops, plus all these exclusive benefits:

- 🌹 FREE home delivery
- 🌹 Exclusive offers and our monthly newsletter
- 🌹 Membership to our special rewards programme

We hope that after receiving your free books you'll want to remain a member. But the choice is yours. So why not give us a go. You'll be glad you did!

Visit www.millsandboon.co.uk for the latest news and offers.

Mrs/Miss/Ms/Mr .... Initials ....
BLOCK CAPITALS PLEASE

Surname ....

Address ....

....

.... Postcode ....

Email ....

P1FIA

The Mills & Boon® Book Club™ – Here's how it works:

Accepting your free books places you under no obligation to buy anything. You may keep the books and gift and return t
despatch note marked 'cancel'. If we do not here from you, about a month later we'll send you 4 brand new stories from
Modern series priced at £3.30* each. That is the complete price – there is no extra charge for post and packaging. You m
cancel at any time, otherwise we will send you 4 stories a month which you may purchase or return to us – the choice
is yours.

*Terms and prices subject to change without notice.

FREE BOOK OFFER

FREEPOST NAT 10298

RICHMOND

TW9 1BR

NO STAMP
NECESSARY
IF POSTED IN
THE U.K. OR N.I.

to consume her. "The proper response is, 'Why yes, Ethan, I think I have.'" He waited while she blinked at him, bewildered and aroused and speechless. At her continued silence, he said, "I see I need to work harder to convince you." His head lowered again, only this time, his hands trailed from her neck to her shoulders, down to her capped sleeves and the band of bare flesh above her gloves. His thumbs, those long, clever thumbs, strayed inward to brush tight, constricting spirals around her peaked nipples.

She reared back with an astonished squeak, gripping his wrists and pressing his hands away while flames heated her face and chest. Frantic, she peered over his shoulder to see if they'd been seen. "You can't do that here!"

The blue in his eyes deepened to cobalt and his wrists slowly rotated within her weakening grip. "Then let's go somewhere where we can."

"Ethan!"

His hands broke free, then rose to grip the sides of her head while dizzy longing and trembling anticipation gathered in her veins. "Tell me you want me," he repeated.

Realizing he'd suffer no compunction at all with seducing her in public, she admitted, "Wanting you is not the issue and you know it."

"Say it anyway," he ordered, tipping her head back until her throat was exposed to his unrelenting command. He pressed a hot kiss against the pulse point in her neck and she shivered. "Let me hear it, Cate."

Too lost in the fire of arousal to resist, she repeated, "I want you."

His mouth tracked a scorching trail along her collarbone, then rose to nip at her earlobe. "How much?"

"Too much." Her hands fluttered up to his head. Dragged his mouth to hers.

He obliged her silent plea with a few more moments of

delicious ravaging that soon had her backed up tight within the corner and her breath coming in short, choppy gasps. She could feel the tensile length of his erection against her abdomen, could feel her own rising need to join with him. He nudged her up onto her toes, his hips grinding a slow, seductive circle against hers. "Let's get out of here," he whispered into her panting mouth.

Alarmed by her lack of control, she pushed against his chest, trying to create space between their fused bodies. Trying to reclaim her equilibrium. *What is he doing to me?* "I can't," she protested, even as her fingers splayed helplessly over the contours of his chest.

"You can." He pressed against her fingers, until the tips of her breasts grazed the backs of her hands. "Come with me. Let me take you away from this place."

She flushed. Pushed harder against his chest. "No. I'm not leaving with you, Ethan. I'm sorry, but I can't. No."

With that, she ducked beneath his arm and dashed back into the crowded studio.

To her consternation, Ethan didn't leave. She was convinced he'd remained just to torture her. By evening's end, she noticed that he'd flirted with nearly every female in attendance. Holding court at the center of the room, he charmed men and women alike with his humor, his smiles and his effortless appeal. He behaved as if having hordes of sighing, panting women fawning at his feet was a normal, everyday occurrence.

The fact that it probably was didn't help Cate's mood one bit.

So when he acknowledged yet another vapid fairy who'd drifted annoyingly close to his side, a flare of possessiveness had Cate glaring daggers at the back of his head. Though she knew she had no claim on him, it irritated her that he'd profess his plans to bed her one minute and then ignore her in favor of every other woman in the room for the rest of the night.

Exasperated by her reaction, Cate deliberately turned away. She'd put in her time at the event; she'd seen the people she needed to see and conversed with those who needed to speak with her. She was ready to return home.

Angry satisfaction suffused her chest and her transparent heels made a lovely, irritated click as she made her way down the empty hallway leading to the coat check room. It wasn't until she reached the empty elbow of the hall that she heard footsteps trailing her. Turning, she discovered that Ethan had followed her into the narrow, poorly lit corridor.

Cate immediately resumed her walking. She quickened her pace, wanting to leave him staring after her the way she'd stared after him all night. But his longer legs had him catching up to her in fewer than ten strides. He reached for her upper arm, his low voice rippling the air beside her cheek. "Leaving so soon?"

She jerked away from his touch and glared up at him. "Yes."

He looked down at his empty hand and a smile gathered behind his eyes. "Why?"

Feeling foolish for the way she'd reacted, she lifted her chin and forced politeness back into her tone. "The night's winding down and I'm tired."

"It's barely eleven and you don't look tired at all."

Cate ground her teeth, knowing he spoke the truth but too embarrassed to acknowledge it. "Do you have a point, Ethan?"

"Of course I do," he said with abominable cheerfulness. "Your leaving has nothing to do with your fatigue and everything to do with me. Admit it."

She rolled her eyes. "Contrary to popular opinion, the world does not revolve around you."

"Then why are you running away from me?"

"I'd have to be chased before I could run away," she blurted without thinking, then immediately wished her accident had damaged her tongue instead of everything else that mattered.

The smile deepened, denting his cheek and fanning lines from the corners of his blue, blue eyes. "Do you want me to chase you?"

"No!" She tried to step past him, but he moved, blocking her escape.

"You sure?"

"Of course," she snapped. She moved right, then left while he remained stubbornly in front of her. "Would you kindly move out of my way?"

"They haven't announced the winners of the costume competition yet," he told her, that beguiling smile of his sending sparks of sensation to her fingertips. "And you've definitely got my vote."

"I don't care about the costume competition," she said in exasperation.

"How are you getting home?" he asked, changing the subject with a swiftness that sparked her suspicions.

"I've called a car. Not that it's any of your business."

"Why don't you let me drive you instead?"

She shot him a speaking glance. "Absolutely not."

"Scared?"

"Pragmatic." She crossed her arms beneath her breasts, scolding him with a glare. "You've shown yourself to be remarkably free of restraint."

"Guilty as charged." He smiled. "But I have the papers in my car," he said. "All signed and ready to go."

"So? Send them to my office."

"I'd rather deliver them in person."

"Go ahead. Janine will be happy to meet with you."

He shook his head. "I want to deliver them to you. In your study."

"Why?"

"Don't tell me you've forgotten already."

Against her better judgment, a small huff of laughter escaped her lips. "You don't give up, do you?"

"Never."

"If I allow you to drive me home, do you promise to stop this crazy attempt to seduce me?"

He placed a hand over his heart and solemnly swore, "I promise. The moment I drop you off at your home, I will consider our business complete."

She studied him through narrowed eyes, debating the truth of his words. He'd never lied to her before, but she still didn't know if it was safe to trust his word. "Fine," she relented. "You drive me home, and we're done. Agreed?"

"Agreed." He extended a hand, palm up. "Do you have your coat check stub?"

She flushed. "Yes."

He waited, his palm hovering between them.

"Turn around and I'll get it."

Without speaking a word, he turned his back so she could retrieve the small ticket from between her breasts. When she met his eyes again, it was to find blue fire sparking in their depths. "What else do you keep in there?" he asked.

Her blush burned brighter and she shoved past him. He caught up with her in two strides, claimed her ticket and within thirty seconds, he'd collected her cream coat from the bored redhead at the coat check room. He threaded Cate's arms through the heavy wool, adjusted the lapels beneath her chin and then placed her gloved hand in the crook of his arm.

He looked down at her, his intent blue eyes sending a hum of longing through her veins. "You look good on my arm, Catydid."

Anticipation skittered through her chest, sending a shiver through her body. "This doesn't mean I've changed my mind about sleeping with you."

His voice deepened while a hint of teasing flirted within his eyes. "I didn't think it had."

Arousal collected in her womb, mingling with the excitement and confusion being with Ethan wrought. Oh, she was truly, truly in trouble.

She wanted him.

And it was getting harder and harder to remember why she shouldn't.

CHAPTER NINE

JUST as Ethan had arranged, the carriage he'd reserved waited for them at the base of the building. The liveried driver dismounted to place a step stool next to the black carriage, sweeping the two of them forward with a bow. Cate's feet stalled for a moment, her narrow hand tugging against his biceps and her eyes widening in surprise. Ethan smiled down at her shocked expression and then ushered her forward again.

He handed her up into the high bench seat, then vaulted up to settle in next to her. After he'd tucked the heavy blanket over her legs, he wrapped his arm around her slim shoulders, tucking her in close. A faint scent of citrus and vanilla tugged at his nostrils, bringing memories of their night together and teasing tightness back into his groin. Determined to take things slow, he took a moment to congratulate himself on yet another step of a plan well executed. By night's end, he'd have her back in his arms, then he'd seduce her so thoroughly she'd never push him away again.

The driver clucked the horse into motion and Cate shifted, pulling back to angle a suspicious glance toward him. "You said you were taking me home," she accused.

"I didn't say when."

"So when did you arrange this carriage?"

The minute you tried to dismiss me with your damn paperwork. "Why?"

"It's a bit premeditated, don't you think?" She smoothed her gloved hands over the blanket as she scolded him from the corner of her eye. "And a little presumptuous for you to just assume I'd say yes."

His unrepentant smile teased a reciprocal grin from her. "Haven't you heard? The best way to achieve your goals is to behave as if you've already met them."

"Hmm." She nodded. "And what, pray tell, would you have done had I kept saying no?"

"I'd have ridden through Central Park all alone, wallowing in solitary misery."

Laughter bubbled from her throat. "You are such a liar! You'd have found a half-dozen willing females—no, make that supermodels—to assuage the pain of your *solitude*."

"Not true." He sobered, holding her gaze. "If I can't have you, I'd rather be alone."

Disbelief marred the clearness of her green eyes while a pretty pink blush rose to stain her cheeks. "Don't be ridiculous."

He feigned a wince. "That's a little harsh, don't you think?"

"It's true!" Chastened, but still insistent, she continued, "You don't even know me anymore. Claiming you'd rather be alone than be without me is crazy!"

"But I do know you, Cate." He cupped his hand around her shoulder, squeezing delicately as he leaned to peruse her defensive expression. "Better than you think I do."

She bit her lip and dropped her gaze. "Ten years ago, maybe. But you don't know me now."

"Don't I?" He lifted his free hand to her downturned chin and tipped her face up. "My success stems from an ability to make split-second decisions about any given opportunity. I've learned to trust my instincts, whether it's with property, investments or people. And my instincts are telling me I want you."

Twin furrows formed between her brows. "But relationships aren't the same as business. There's more to human interaction than investment potential and the bottom line."

"I disagree," he told her. "There's always a bottom line, whether monetary or not. And with you, I'm willing to negotiate for the pleasure I know we could share."

"Negotiate!" She gaped at him as if he'd just spoken in tongues. "I don't care how much money or property you have or how many businesses you run. You're still a person. A human being. And human beings don't interact this way."

"Of course they do. Whether you admit it or not, every relationship is just a series of negotiated business transactions. Physical pleasure, time, prestige and emotion are the currency we use to barter for what we want. Why ignore that reality, instead of using it to our benefit?"

She reared away from his touch. "No wonder you burn through women like you do. No self-respecting female could withstand that attitude for long."

"You might think so," he said reasonably. "But you'd be wrong. Every one of them has begged to stay."

"Well," she said, crossing her arms over her ribs, "I guess I have more self-respect than they do, don't I?"

"Which is why I'm so intrigued."

"Exactly. What kind of fool would I be if I allowed you to seduce me, only to pay the price when you've had your fill?"

He cocked his head and smiled. "See? Even you use the language of business to assess the risk."

"Only because for you, it would be business. A cold, calculated transaction in flesh that would leave me miserable and hurting."

"You flatter me, sweet. To think I'd have the power to hurt you. Who knew?"

"Don't be like that, Ethan."

"Like what?"

"Sarcastic and mean." She studied him with a perplexed little frown. "Why are you so hard now?"

Because you ripped my heart out and left me to bleed. "I prefer to think of it as smart."

"Smart?" Sadness, or maybe it was even regret, softened her green eyes as she stared at him. "You forget, Ethan. I know what's beneath that shell you've built around yourself. I know you, and you're not like this."

An uncomfortable ache fisted within his chest, but he kept his expression impassive. "Now look who's claiming to know the other, despite ten long years of separation."

Her eyes narrowed as she turned on the seat to face him. "Can I ask you something?"

The frisson of unease coiled even tighter in his gut. "Depends."

"Have you loved even one of those other women you've so callously discarded?"

"They knew the terms before becoming involved."

"You're avoiding the question."

"Does it matter?"

"I wouldn't ask if it didn't."

He glared at her, not liking the way she'd derailed the conversation. He'd planned to seduce her, to overcome her resistance with carefully orchestrated romance and blinding pleasure. He'd planned to ravage her, to make her vulnerable without losing one atom of his own control. Discussing *love* had never been on his agenda. "Love is a marketing ploy used to sell flowers and cards to the gullible masses," he bit out.

"I'll take that as a no, then."

"Love just makes people miserable. I have no interest in it."

"Because of what I did to you?"

He forcibly relaxed the tension in his jaw and hands. "No,

Cate." He infused the words with a hint of rebuke. "Because I grew up."

Her expression, soft and filled with remorse, told him she knew he lied. "I'm sorry I made you afraid of love."

A flare of irritation gathered ground, making him forget his plans for a slow, deliberate seduction. He wanted to hurt her *now*, to punish her for refusing to acknowledge that *he* held the upper hand and that his emotional barometer was no longer calibrated to her feelings toward him. "I'm not afraid of love."

"Then why are you still alone?"

"Why are you?" he shot back.

She sucked in a breath, her glorious emerald eyes looking wounded. Bruised.

Steeling himself against the urge to pull her close and apologize, he said, "Can't handle it when the questions are aimed at you, huh?"

For a moment, she simply stared at him, looking both bereft and defiant at the same time. "I'm alone because I want it all," she finally said. "I want a family and security and someone to come home to at night. I want a reason to smile, a reason to get up in the morning and a purpose to give my life meaning. I want someone to love me unconditionally. And even knowing I can't ever have it, I'm not willing to settle for anything less." She lifted her chin, her trembling mouth and wavering voice tugging hard against his better judgment. "What's your excuse?"

"I don't need one," he said, brutally quashing the need to comfort her. "I have everything I want, and am perfectly content with my life as it is."

"Then why are you pursuing me?"

He glowered at her in silence.

"If you're perfectly content, why court the messiness I'm sure to bring?" Her cheeks flared with distressed color as she pressed her point. "With our history, with all the ugly baggage of our past, why on earth would you choose to seduce me over the dozens of other women you could have without any strings attached?"

"Because."

"Because?" She huffed out an exasperated exhale. "How is that a reason?"

"I don't know," he snapped. "Maybe I want to prove that I'm good enough to claim you."

The words hung suspended between them, revealing far more than he'd intended to reveal. But it was too late to call them back, too late to stuff them back inside, deep, deep inside where they belonged.

Cate stared at Ethan, the vulnerability beneath his admission making her ache for the man he'd once been, for the man he'd hidden away from the world. From himself, even. "Oh, Ethan," she said softly, lifting a palm to his face while her eyes searched his. "You were always good enough for me. How could you ever doubt that?"

He lifted his chin from her hand and glared out over their liveried driver's head. "Spare me your damn pity."

"What?"

He dismissed her question with a scowl, his jaw bunching in anger.

"It's not pity," she insisted. "Why on earth would you think I pity you?"

When he ignored her in favor of the passing city lights leading to the park, she stopped pressing for answers and simply watched him in silence. Tension radiated off of him, knit into his clenched teeth and rigid thighs and arms. His posture alone testified to the emotional walls he'd erected, keeping him guarded and alone. It made her want to pull him close, wrap her arms around him and tuck herself up against his ribs. She wanted to warm the coldness inside, to comfort him and convince him of his own worth.

"The park is beautiful," she finally said, once they'd entered the canopy of trees lining the main drive within Central Park.

"It is," he said in curt agreement.

It wasn't much, but it was a start. She ran a finger over a seam in the blanket, close to his thigh but not quite touching. "I'd forgotten how good it smells here."

He didn't reply and her words died to silence on the cold October breeze. Overhead, trees interlaced their shadowed branches, allowing intermittent views of a star-studded sky. After a while, she reached for his hand, curling her gloved fingers over his clenched fist. He remained stiff and unyielding until, feeling foolish, she moved to withdraw her touch.

"Don't," he said, breaking the silence. He turned his hand to claim hers and then dragged their joined fingers to his hard thigh. Despite the cold, he was warm, seeping heat through her long, white glove.

"Ethan—"

"Don't talk," he said without looking at her, his hand tightening around hers. "Just enjoy the drive."

She nodded in mute agreement, a fragile hope winging through her chest. Maybe now, they could move forward. Without any barriers. Without any lies.

As they made their leisurely circuit around the park with their hands joined, her hopes tightened into an unbearable knot of longing. It felt as if they were the only two people in the park, alone in a wooded wonderland while the rest of the world spun crazily around them.

After a few more minutes of silence, broken only by the steady rhythm of the horse's hooves, Ethan divested Cate of her glove. Their bare hands met, palm against palm beneath the blanket, and she closed her eyes, steeping herself in his nearness. His thumb grazed the edge of hers for a while, ratcheting up the aching need that had settled into her stomach.

Tucked up against him with the scents of fall mingling with his masculine essence, she could almost pretend they were lovers in truth. She could almost pretend that her scars wouldn't matter and that the past ten years had never happened.

CHAPTER TEN

WHEN the carriage driver drew to a halt several blocks outside the park, Cate recognized the location and then turned to Ethan with a curious, surprised glance. "What are we doing here?"

"I'm hungry." His glance grazed her mouth.

"But aren't they closed?"

"Not to us." He handed her down from the carriage. "When's the last time you ate a decent meal?"

Certainly not in the past few days. She hadn't eaten properly before the auction, as her nerves had been too highly strung. And in the wake of his seduction, she'd been too distracted to think about food. Too nervous and unsettled. "Yesterday?" she said, realizing she was famished.

Ethan pressed his mouth into a grim line of disapproval. Within minutes, he'd escorted her inside Le Bernardin's elegant dining room.

"There's no one else here!" Cate gasped, turning to view the restaurant's interior, empty save for their sole table.

"I met the chef at your auction," Ethan said, as if he reserved entire restaurants after hours as a matter of course. "He agreed to provide an intimate meal for two at my behest."

"I'm impressed." She relinquished her coat and slid into the silk-covered seat before a waiter materialized to drape a linen napkin over her lap.

An hour and a half later, after being spoiled by the flawless French service, an incomparable sommelier, a lovely shrimp ravioli puddled in truffle sauce and two full glasses of wine, Cate realized the heated emotion infusing her was more than mere tipsiness. Ethan had relaxed over dinner, losing much of the hard, defensive edge he'd worn in the park, and it made her harbor hopes she had no business feeling. Hopes that she felt nonetheless.

"Tell me about Europe," she said, leaning forward to cup her chin within her palm. "Do you have a special project that means more to you than the others?"

"Every businessman remembers his first success," he said, looking at her over his glass of wine. "That first moment when he starts to believe he can actually catch the dream he's been chasing."

"That was your first hotel in London, right?"

He nodded, a small smile flirting with his mouth. "The first one I financed and built all on my own, yes."

"I read somewhere that you've built a hundred since."

"One hundred and eight." His eyes flashed with pride and she felt her own heart welling with reciprocal satisfaction.

"But none in the States yet."

"Not yet," he said cryptically. "But I'm considering a hotel here, in New York."

"So you might come back? For more than just this trip?"

His gaze caught hers and held. "Depends," he said.

A flutter of awareness beat low within her belly. "On what?"

"You."

She swallowed, the wine in her stomach heating with a surge of longing. Maybe she could snatch a few hours of pleasure before fate ripped Ethan away again. Maybe she could wrest a little joy from the barren future stretched ahead of her. Didn't she owe it to herself to glean as much happiness as possible before the truth sent him away again?

Slightly tipsy, more than slightly aroused and starved for another of his bold kisses, Cate fantasized about how the night might unfold. With him. In the dark. In his bed.

What if they could make love without him seeing her scars? Without pity and disgust and regrets about the past rising up between them? She knew she couldn't postpone the inevitable forever, but maybe, for a couple of idyllic hours, she could forget all the reasons things would never work between them.

They shared a decadent chocolate-chicory dessert and he watched her with burning eyes as she licked the final bit of chocolate *cremeux* from her thumb. Staring over the flickering candlelight on their table, she leaned forward to run her fingers around the base of her wineglass, a mere hairsbreadth from Ethan's splayed hand. Her eyes drifted halfway shut as the quiet night closed around them, until the only sounds were their unsteady breaths.

He moved his hand so his fingertips brushed the ridge of her knuckles. "Ready?"

"Yes." Desire hung between them, thick and intoxicating, and she wondered how he'd react, were she to lift her stocking-clad foot between his hard thighs. She wanted, oh, how she wanted, to launch herself onto his lap and feel him against her skin again. "And just so you know…I've changed my mind," she heard herself confess. Emboldened by her own daring, she leaned forward to clarify, "About taking you to my bed."

His fingers froze atop her hand, the shock of his response hovering in the air. He waited ten heartbeats before he slowly exhaled. "You're a little drunk," he finally said, extending his palm and standing. "Aren't you?"

"Maybe," she recklessly admitted, lifting her hand to his. "Does that bother you?"

His profile was shadowed as he pulled her to her feet and then directed her toward the small coatroom to collect her wrap. Ethan helped her into her coat and then curled his hands into her lapels before staring intently into her eyes. "It makes me wonder about your judgment."

A fluttering nervousness beat against her throat. "I'm pretty sure I have none left to wonder about."

He didn't reply. Instead, he led her outside, one hand braced at the base of her spine, the other curved gently around her elbow. After reaching the sidewalk, they were soon swallowed by the glittering night lights of the city.

Times Square was still alive despite the late hour, and inebriated Halloween revelers filled the streets. Some sang, some danced dizzily and still others took advantage of the festive atmosphere to indulge in sloppy public kisses. She shivered and Ethan drew her closer, his voice soft and warm against her ear. "Maybe we should walk a bit."

"Okay," she told him, leaning close to seek refuge from the cold. His tuxedo jacket carried the scents of fall and wine, coupled with the subtle aroma of a virile, aroused man. She could feel his heat, swallowing her up as fully as the surrounding night. As her eyes adjusted to the scene of revelry, Ethan's surefooted steps guided her through the intoxicated crowd.

When she stumbled over a ridge of uneven sidewalk, he anchored his arm about her ribs, bracing her shoulder against his side. "Thank you," she said with a grimace toward her transparent heels. "Cinderella apparently didn't do much walking about the uneven sidewalks of New York."

"Certainly not a tipsy Cinderella," he agreed.

"Then it's a good thing I have you here to save me, huh?"

Ethan stopped, then turned her to face him with a steadying grip against her upper arms. He waited until she raised her eyes to his and then said, "I'm no prince, Cate. You best know that now."

"Oh, I do," she told him before she licked her lips and lowered her gaze to his mouth. "You're my wounded knight, hurting and angry at the world." She leaned forward within his grasp, trying to narrow the distance between them. "You're closed off and emotionally unavailable and I don't care. I want you anyway."

His fingers tightened, his thumbs scant inches from her breasts. The thought of him caressing her there, in all the sensitive places his hands had explored when they were young, made her breath quicken. She stared at him, adrift with longing, until the crests of his cheeks darkened and his nostrils flared. Sure that he'd kiss her again, she swayed toward him and her eyelids fluttered closed.

Instead, he pressed her upright again, dug out his cell phone, dialed and issued a low-voiced order. Snapping it closed, he returned it to his pocket and then guided her into a department store alcove, away from the chilling breeze. The lights of Times Square refracted off the chrome and glass, drawing lines on his lean cheek and casting his profile in shadows. "My car will be here in two minutes."

"I don't mind waiting." She rotated toward his chest and burrowed close, snaking her arms beneath his tuxedo jacket.

Ethan allowed her embrace, gradually relaxing as his breath skimmed the top of her head. They stood in silence for several beats as he scanned the street for his car until it arrived, gliding to a smooth, silent stop. With a subtle press of his palm against her spine, Ethan assisted her into the limousine. The shadowed interior smelled like him, and she inhaled sharply as she slid over the soft, heated leather.

After he'd joined her and the car rejoined the traffic, Cate gathered her courage and twisted until her knee pressed against his hard thigh. Leaning forward, her gaze traced his harsh profile while the lights of the city created moving strips of visibility along his silhouette. Trembling with a mix of fear and daring, she reached for his rigid shoulder. "Will you stay tonight?" she asked. "Once you take me home?"

When he didn't move away, she slid her free hand into the gap between his lapels, beneath the warm weight of wool, and skimmed her fingers down the shirt and vest of his tuxedo. The muscles of his chest flexed beneath her palm.

"I'd like you to," she told him. She shifted her hand until the insistent clubbing of his heart abraded her palm. "I'd like to spend a night with you."

Ethan remained still, his fists knotted against his thighs. "Cate."

"Please," she urged. "I want to…" Cate slid closer to him, both hands shoving the sleek tuxedo jacket aside so she could work on the buttons of his vest and shirt. He did nothing to help her, as she quickly worked from his throat down to the waistband of his pants. Shaking with nervousness, she sucked in a hot breath when her fingertips finally came into contact with his fever-hot skin.

Excitement seared her as she pulled his shirt free and then spread it wide to her greedy fingers. Her palms itched to explore the shadowed textures, and she succumbed to the desire, dragging her sensitive palms down the scented, tantalizing stretch of taut skin and springy hair. Fervent determination fired her blood as she found his flat nipple with her fingertip. Expecting him to push her back at any moment, she leaned forward to graze it with her tongue.

Ethan groaned and his chest heaved beneath her questing mouth. He tunneled his fingers along her scalp and wrenched her head away from his skin, hauling her up until his mouth caught hers in a voracious, drugging kiss. Hard shivers wracked Cate's body while his hands moved from her head to her hips. Lifting her, he positioned her buttocks over his spraddled thighs before he returned his attentions to her mouth. Several long moments later, his breath choppy and raw, he withdrew enough to stare at the stiff corset of her Cinderella costume.

The boned velvet pushed her breasts high, creating cleavage that now captured his hungry gaze. Awash with a surreal sense of bravery, she reached for his hands and pulled them to her chest. His eyes flashed hot before he twisted his wrists to brush his fingers in a reverent arc over each shadowed curve. He dipped to kiss the plump top of her left breast, then hooked a thumb over the edge of her corset and bra, bending both down until her pebbled nipple popped free.

Bared to him now, she waited, her breath suspended, until he leaned to trace the ruched areola, then the puckered tip, with his tongue. Currents of sensation shot to her core. She arched and gasped as he sucked her deep into his hot mouth, desire thrumming insistently through every cell of her body as she clutched the back of his head and pulled him even closer. When he released her with a damp waft of breath, his teeth flashed white until she twisted and moaned for more. He obliged by bending to her other side, his tongue pulling desire from deep within.

She throbbed. She wanted. She needed… Oh, he rolled the exquisitely taut peak between his teeth, scissoring with feathery, delicate pressure that sent arrows of arousal to every nerve ending. Cate was so hypnotized by the pleasure of his ministrations that she didn't notice he'd shoved her gown up until the hard press of his bare hand against her buttocks had her arching against his long, hard erection. Breath hissed through his teeth as she ground into the tight ridge thickening the front of his tuxedo pants.

Mindless to the pleasure rocketing through her, Cate flung her arms around his neck and dragged her mouth over the thrumming pulse beneath his jaw. She pressed her bared breasts against his hard chest, squirming to get closer. He gripped her head, seized her mouth in a marauding kiss, then wrenched away with a low mutter. "Cover yourself," he said.

"What?" Disoriented, she automatically acquiesced as he crossed her cloak over her exposed breasts.

"We're here." His eyes, dark and glinting, promised to continue where they'd left off. "And I'd rather Walter not see you like this."

Awkwardly, she scrambled off his lap, shoving her feet into her discarded shoes. By the time Ethan's chauffeur opened the door, she'd restored some semblance of order to her disheveled costume if not to her flushed skin and dismantled hair.

The man averted his eyes and handed her out onto the cement walkway, doffing his hat as Ethan emerged behind her.

"Thank you, Walter," Ethan said.

"Yes, sir."

By the time the chauffeur had rounded the sleek black car, Ethan had already ushered her out onto the empty tarmac of a private airstrip. A white jet stood at the ready, her pilot circling its nose to check the far wing. An abrupt surge of nervousness sent Cate's heart into a thudding tailspin while a trickle of sweat beaded between her breasts. She stood, frozen, unable to make her feet move while Ethan pressed an arm against her back and urged her forward.

No longer awash in dreamy fantasy, reality slapped against her consciousness with brutal clarity. Waves of heat and ice sliced through her as she turned to meet his gaze. His eyes were bright in the runway lights. The piercing blue hooded beneath a fan of black lashes brought back the searing memory of her writhing greedily against him in his limo, their mouths feasting on one another while her desire for pleasure, for darkness, had blinded her to the dangers ahead.

Unsettled, Cate adjusted her coat and inhaled thinly through her nostrils while pricks of heat blossomed on her face. He continued to stare down at her, his eyes filled with a disquieting glint of command.

"What are we doing here?" she asked, though she knew with a sickening certainty what his reply would be.

"We're flying to the island."

Fingers of panic wrapped around her heart, squeezing hard. "I never agreed to that."

"You said you wanted a night with me."

"I meant here. In New York."

"But the island will be better," he said softly, his eyes glittering with immutable intent. "It'll bring us full circle."

She'd braced herself for his rejection, had told herself she could handle the risk to her heart if it meant a few hours of pleasure with the man she'd once loved. She could handle him discovering her secrets, could withstand his rejection once he saw her scars. Here, in New York, with its cold October breezes, crazy social calendar and bustling anonymity, she could lie to herself and pretend the pain away once he pushed her away. She could survive.

But being alone with him on the island paradise of their youth while he stripped her soul bare? "No," she snapped, a panicked nervousness making it hard to breathe. "I can't."

"Why not?"

Her chilled hands grew damp within her gloves and she spun toward the safety of the limousine. But Walter had already started pulling away. She wanted to run after him, to slap at the windows and beg until he stopped and allowed her back inside. "I can't," she repeated, her voice thin with fear.

Ethan stared at her with a flicker of surprise. "You're scared."

Ducking her head while terror channeled through her, she nodded. "I'm sorry," she confessed through chattering teeth. "It's just that I haven't been there since... And I...we..." She trailed off, miserable and afraid.

"Cate. You're overreacting." His hand cupped her elbow and tugged, pulling her toward the small jet staircase. "Come."

Too overcome to wage a decent verbal defense, she wrenched her arm free and shook her head jerkily. "No. I can't."

"Why?"

"Because." She inhaled sharply, readjusting her expectations of the night, reminding herself of why it had been foolish to hope for something that could never be. "I just want to go home. You said you'd take me home."

"I will." He reclaimed her arm, ushering her closer to the airplane's waiting staircase. "After the island."

"No."

He maintained his grip, moving to tower over her despite her protests. "Yes."

"I was tipsy," she blurted. "I extended an invitation I shouldn't have. Surely you don't intend to kidnap me because of it!"

"This has nothing to do with the wine or your invitation, Cate."

"Then what? Why are you forcing me to come to the island with you?"

Ethan's gaze flattened and his fingers tightened against her biceps. "Because you owe me."

"I owe you?" she shouted. "What are you talking about?"

"There was no internship."

It took a few seconds for his words to register. "No intern—what?" She felt the blood drain from her face.

Refusing to grant her refuge from the truth, he held her gaze. "The internship with Stevenson and Sons that your father supposedly set up for me? It didn't exist." A grim smile curved his mouth. "Unless, of course, you consider being beaten within an inch of my life the moment I showed up to claim it an *internship*."

Her mouth moved soundlessly as she processed his revelation.

"Your father lied to you, Cate, so you'd break things off with me. He played us both because he didn't like a lowly manual laborer sniffing around his daughter. And you believed his lies because it was easier to reject me than to defy your own father."

"That's not why," she whispered.

"Does it matter?"

A paralyzing shame tweaked the back of Cate's neck. How could she have not seen it, knowing how proud her father was, how focused he was on prestige and wealth? Every muscle in her body drew into uncomfortable tautness, flogging her with guilty recriminations and agonizing what-ifs. "Ethan, I…" she gasped. "Oh, God. No wonder you're so angry. No wonder you hate me."

His face remained an inscrutable mask. "I don't hate you."

"You have to believe me! I never would have sent you away, had I known!"

"But you did, didn't you?" He dropped his gaze to her mouth, then leisurely returned to her eyes. "Which is why you're going to come to the island with me. Tonight."

Suddenly, the promise she'd wrung from Ethan so long ago came back to haunt her with bruising clarity.

"Promise you won't leave me, Ethan."

"You don't have to ask."

"Say it anyway. I need to hear it."

"I promise. I love you. Of course I'll never leave you."

She'd believed him, had known he loved her more than

he loved himself. Time and time again, he'd whispered his devotion, his love, his commitment. And because of that, she'd known the only way to make him leave was to convince him that she no longer wanted him.

She pressed trembling hands against her stomach, guilt coiling in her chest like a living thing. She'd treated him so terribly. And he'd believed her lies. To give him a future, she'd killed his love for her. And for what? An internship that had never existed?

He must have taken her silence as acquiescence, because he escorted her the remaining distance without resistance. Her pulse rioted like an undisciplined child's as he guided her up the small flight of steps and ushered her into the spacious cabin. When he ducked in after her, the space seemed to shrink. His large, broad body filled the room and stole all the air.

She couldn't breathe. Couldn't move.

"Cate," he said in a low voice against her ear.

Lurching forward, she stumbled into the window seat and then gripped the armrests with trembling, fumbling hands. She dragged in several deep, cleansing breaths, like those she'd used for so many years during her physical therapy, like those she'd learned to use in preparation for pain.

As much as the seat belt would allow, she angled herself toward the window and stared out onto the empty tarmac. The double layer of glass misted beneath her breath, blurring the city's landscape. Breathing deeply, she splayed her fingers against the cold glass and willed herself to calm. For Ethan, she could make it through whatever came next; she could survive. She could wall up her vulnerable heart and withstand the devastation of her most cherished memories. She'd be battered and wounded, but she'd live.

Oblivious to her inner turmoil, Ethan exchanged a few quiet words with the pilot and then settled in next to her.

Despite the layers of wool and velvet between their adjacent thighs, she felt his heat. She smelled his scent, the drugging combination of cologne, soap and virile male. Being in such close quarters, knowing the pain she'd caused him, made her feel jittery.

The feelings only magnified as the plane took to the air and the cabin pressure changed, echoing the dizzying imbalance within her chest.

When they reached a cruising altitude, Ethan's voice broke the silence. "It's only for one day," he said quietly. "While I get the specs to remodel for Dad."

She swallowed and said nothing.

His head bent toward hers until his breath stirred the hair at her temple. One of his square hands moved to stroke the side of her neck, brushing the skin beneath her ear with a feathery touch. "I want new memories, Cate. Memories of you and me, together, on the island as equals."

Aching tendrils of regret snaked through her belly as she nodded, bringing a burn of tears to the back of her throat. What he didn't know was that those memories had been the only thing that kept her sane. In those years of debilitating pain, the memories of his love had kept her fighting and alive. She couldn't bear to replace them with the harsh, bitter reality of her future. Of the woman she'd become. She couldn't bear the reminder of what she'd lost.

CHAPTER ELEVEN

By THE time they arrived at Grantley Adams in Barbados, Ethan had watched Cate stare nervously out the window for nearly three hours. Worry pleated her brow and knotted her fingers, muddying his motives and making him want to soothe her fears. But didn't he want her uncomfortable? Didn't he want her off kilter and in pain?

His reactions didn't make any sense. He shouldn't yearn to protect her, to keep her safe. Even so, the urge to stroke her satiny skin, to explore the petal-softness of her jaw and long, thin neck had roared through him to the point that he'd had to join his pilot in the cockpit to keep from touching her. Kissing her. Soothing her and loving her and making her his in every way possible.

Ethan's pilot had called ahead to schedule transportation to the island, so within another hour, they and the luggage Ethan had packed for them both had been delivered to the small dock just outside the Carrington beach house.

"It looks the same, doesn't it?" he asked. The sunrise glinted gold and pink against the brilliant blue of the sea, momentarily blinding Ethan. He felt dawn's rising heat beat upon his shoulders, a welcome change from the New York chill.

"Yes," she agreed as they watched the boat depart. Cate had shed her coat, and stood in her wrinkled Cinderella costume, her rumpled hair drifting in the breeze. She turned, lifting a hand to shade her anxious eyes, and peered along the northern shore.

His gaze followed hers, snagging on the large, partially concealed rock while a wash of memories flooded him: Cate, sprawled lazily atop its sun-warmed surface while he stole peeks at her budding breasts; fresh pomegranate juice dribbling down her chin and forearm, trails of sticky sweetness he'd longed to lick from her skin during one of their clandestine midnight picnics; listening to katydids sing while he brushed his fingers close to her bare thigh and silently charted their future in the stars above.

"I wonder if my shell collection is still over there."

He eased out a tight exhale, remembering the way she'd sorted his forfeited shells, remembering the sweet torture of banked passion. Realizing that even though he'd taken her fully less than forty-eight hours ago, it wasn't enough. It would never be enough. "I can't imagine who would have moved it."

"We didn't hire anyone to replace you and your father after you left," Cate told him as she turned toward the house. "I expect the grounds will be quite overgrown."

Ethan cleared his throat. He couldn't allow the sounds and scents of the island to undermine his resolve to remain aloof. Separate. Cold. He'd brought Cate here to make her vulnerable, not to drown in the past himself. "That's okay. I figure it'll keep Dad busy." Ethan squinted toward the empty house and caretaker's cottage. "Make him realize how much he's needed here."

When she didn't answer, Ethan lifted the suitcases he'd packed. He began the trek back to the main house, his shoes crunching against the broken shell walkway while she trailed behind him.

The beach house, a symphony of emerald-green vines,

colonial finials and white-washed clapboard, glinted on the pathway ahead. Weathered by decades of sand and sun, the two-story beach retreat belonged in the landscape of Ethan's memories as much as Cate did. As they approached, Ethan's eyes involuntarily rose to the trio of white-curtained windows on the second story.

Cate's windows.

He remembered all the times he'd snuck up to her breezy balcony just to watch her sleep. All the times he'd climbed that crosshatch of vines, risking a painful fall and an outraged dismissal, just on the off chance that Cate might be awake. Up for a nighttime adventure. Or another stolen kiss.

Dismissing the memories that brought an unwelcome softening of his resolve, he hauled in a breath and stepped over the threshold. No longer the servant, no longer barred entry to the sacred enclave of the privileged, he entered the house as its owner.

He expected it to feel better.

He expected a sense of triumph. Of victory.

So why did an odd sense of unease rob the satisfaction he should have felt? Why couldn't he revel in his plan, so well-conceived and flawlessly executed that he was exactly where he'd planned to be?

"Ethan," Cate said, interrupting his thoughts. "How is the house so clean?"

"I had it taken care of last week."

"Last week?" Cate followed him up the narrow flight of stairs and into her room, a frothy combination of white cotton, bleached pine furniture and sisal rugs. "But you didn't even bid on the island until two days ago."

"I knew the island was up for auction and I knew it would be mine. I didn't care about the cost."

She stared at him in stunned silence.

"You remember Leon from Flatt's Village, don't you? I

called him and he sent his daughters over to get everything ready." He moved into the room she'd always used and lowered one of the suitcases to the floor.

"That's not mine," she said.

"I packed it for you," Ethan told her. "You can't wear that Cinderella costume all day."

"When did you get my things?"

"I didn't. I went shopping."

"Without knowing my size?"

He stared at her, his chest full of predatory knowledge. "I know your size."

A blush tinted her skin a delectable pink and she averted her gaze.

"I told Dad he gets the master suite, so for now, I'll take this room." He strode across the narrow hallway and into what must have been for guests. It, too, was decorated in simple, clean lines that welcomed the soft breezes from the sea. Like Cate's, it boasted a king-sized bed with enough room beneath its waist-high mattress to host a small dinner party. Sheer white curtains billowed inward from tall windows, and he detected the faint bite of salt water in the air. Turning, he noticed that he could see Cate standing at the foot of her equally white, equally tempting bed from his doorway.

He wondered which set of sheets they'd be messing up first.

"Cate?" he called, swinging his own suitcase onto the bed and then turning to face her. "You up for a swim?"

She froze, raising startled eyes to his. "What?"

"A swim. Would you rather go now or later?"

Biting her lower lip, she shook her head. "Neither. I don't have a suit."

"Yes, you do." He gestured toward the suitcase he'd packed for her. "I threw in a couple of bikinis that should fit."

He unzipped his luggage and leaned to snag the blue trunks

and a white T-shirt he'd packed, then turned to find Cate's face blanched of all color.

White as the sand outside, she looked ready to faint. "Cate?" he asked, striding across the hallway and into her room. "What is it?"

She started. Stretched her mouth into a thin, scared smile. "Nothing."

Ethan regarded her quietly, unnerved by the fear that widened her eyes and made her lips go pale. He reached for her cold, trembling hand and lifted it between them. "Cate."

"It's nothing." Shallow breaths lifted her ribs in rapid succession, doing nothing to alleviate her stricken expression. "I just don't want to go swimming."

His eyes narrowed as he studied her face. "You love swimming."

"Not anymore," she said, trying to tug free as she stared over his shoulder toward the doorway. "But you go on without me," she insisted. "I'll be fine here."

He refused to release her, trying to reclaim her focus. After a gentle jostling had no effect, he tipped her chin until she met his eyes. "Does this have anything to do with your accident?" he asked softly.

Cate's eyes widened and she yanked away from him, jerking backward and whacking her elbow against the thick bedpost. She winced and pulled her elbow into her cupped hand. "What does my accident have to do with anything?"

"You tell me."

"There's nothing to tell," she said, retreating behind the bedpost and the wall of white mattress between them. "And even if there were, I wouldn't want to talk about it."

"Why not?" he asked, following her around to the side of her bed.

She inched even farther away. "Because it's none of your business."

Seeing her wary expression and the telltale signs of her avoidance, Ethan felt frustration rise within his chest. She was hiding from him. Throwing up barriers of half truths and lies. Still. Narrowing his gaze, he studied the taut lines of her face. "Weren't you the one who said you hated lying to me?"

Pink stained her throat and cheeks as she avoided his eyes. "I'm not lying."

Her denial turned his frustration to a simmering anger. "No?"

"No." She lifted her chin, angling her face and torso until all he could see was her profile. "Keeping a secret isn't the same as lying."

"The hell it isn't." He stepped closer, trying to compel her confession by invading her space. "I want the truth. All of it."

"No." She squared her shoulders and turned even farther. Lifting one arm, she placed her small hand flat against the mattress. As if that narrow, sculpted limb created a barrier he wouldn't dare to cross. "I gave you my virginity and I let you bully me into coming here when I didn't want to come. But I won't give you this, so don't ask."

"Don't ask?" he ground out, plucking her hand from the bed and spinning her to face him. "After all the lies you've told, you think I'm just going to back off now?"

She stiffened and then stumbled back, wrenching her wrist from his grasp. "Yes!"

He followed her, crowding her against the wall while her expression filled with distress. "No."

Her nostrils flared while her eyes darted frantically in her efforts to avoid his. "Stop it!"

Anger beat hard within his chest, deepening his voice into its most dangerous register. "Tell me."

Desperation, sharpened by a hint of fear, colored her tone as she bellowed, "Why are you doing this to me?"

"Because I have to know, damn it!" He slammed his palm against the wall beside her head. "I deserve the truth!"

"Fine!" Cate shouted. "I nearly died! Are you happy now?"

Ethan felt the air freeze in his chest and his body went numb. As much as he'd told himself he wanted revenge, the thought of a world without Cate in it made him go cold. "What?"

"You heard me." Inhaling sharply, she lifted her chin and knotted her fists against her thighs. "At times, it hurt so bad, I wished I had."

He wanted to haul her into his arms, to wrap her up next to his chest, absorb her pain and promise to keep her safe forever. But he remained still. Tense and waiting. "Why?"

After another shuddering inhale, she continued, "Because you were gone."

The admission caught him by the throat. Paralyzed his lungs.

"After you left, I didn't care about anything anymore. I loved you and you were gone, so what did it matter? Winning or losing, living or dying, I didn't care."

Worry and fear and regret coiled deep in his gut, an uncomfortable mix of emotions he hadn't expected. Hadn't wanted. Lowering his tingling fingers, desperate to give her comfort, he reached for her tight, bunched shoulder. "I didn't know."

"Don't." She lurched sideways, the thin shield of strength she'd erected seeming almost as fragile as the delicate bones of her body. "I can't handle you touching me right now."

His hands dropped to his sides, knotting into impotent fists against his thighs as he watched her battle her vulnerability to him. Hearing that she'd grieved over him, that she'd loved him enough that she hadn't wanted to live without him, made him realize he'd built his revenge on quicksand.

After she'd sent him away, he'd told himself Cate had never

cared for him. That she'd dabbled with the boy who was beneath her, then grown tired of stringing him along. He'd felt
like an inconvenience. An embarrassment. And even after
she'd confessed her reasons for sending him away, he still
hadn't believed her. He'd chafed under the conviction that
he'd been her first charity project gone awry.

He'd never considered that she might have actually loved
him.

Or that sending him away had hurt her as much as it had
wounded him.

The idea that he might have been wrong all along made him
lose his bearings and set his compass all askew. He reeled,
disoriented and aching with a loss he couldn't articulate. "I'm
sorry," he finally managed.

With her arms wrapped tightly across her ribs, Cate nodded
while her chin trembled beneath the defensive knot of her
mouth.

Silence spun out between them as he waited, his fists
clenched and his lungs aching. "Tell me what happened."

CHAPTER TWELVE

"WHAT would be the point?" Cate inhaled, feeling raw and seared and exposed. "It's in the past."

"I want to understand."

"Fine." Unable to meet his eyes, she stared at the wide plank flooring between her feet. Mustering her courage, knowing full well that the truth would make her vulnerable in a way she'd never been before, she didn't quite know how to start. Yet she pressed forward, girding herself against the pain of her revelation and his reaction to it. "The jumping accident you asked about, the one I had the month you left…"

His expectant silence urged her to continue.

"It wasn't as minor as I led you to believe…" Her hands knotted, the fingernails pressing against the tender flesh of her palms. "It was worse than you could imagine…"

He waited wordlessly as her uneven breaths beat the air between them.

"To escape my grief over losing you, I took a jump I shouldn't have on one of Father's horses." She pulled her lips in and inhaled unsteadily before she resumed. "We didn't make it."

"What happened?"

"We had to put the horse down. And I…well, sometimes I think they should have done the same to me. I crushed my pelvis, damaged multiple internal organs and cracked several vertebrae. According to all the medical professionals, it was a miracle that I wasn't killed or paralyzed."

Risking a glance at Ethan, she saw that his posture had grown even tenser. His knuckles had gone white and he seemed to be tilted slightly forward, his eyes a blaze of blue fire in his taut face.

"But the trade-off for my survival was that I had to undergo countless surgeries and years of excruciating pain." Unable to continue while looking at him, she yanked her gaze aside once more. "Some days, it hurt so much that I wanted nothing more than to give up. I didn't care about walking or living or eating. I didn't care about anything. But about a year after my accident, Mrs. Bartholomew convinced me I should keep trying. That it'd be worth it to live." The memory of that bittersweet day washed over her, and her eyes blurred.

"What did she say?" he asked in a hoarse voice.

Cate hiked her chin, swallowing back a surge of tears she refused to shed. "She showed me an article about you. She'd found it online in some obscure London paper, and though it didn't offer many details, it gave me hope. It made me realize I hadn't been wrong about you. You were succeeding. My sacrifice had made it possible for you to be happy. And reading that, knowing that you were living the dream I wanted you to have, made me feel like it had all been worth it. The pain. The loss. Everything. You were happy, and that was all that mattered." Her words trailed off into silence, though her gaze grimly refused to release his.

Ethan made a suffocated sound, breathing as if someone had knocked the wind out of him.

"Nothing about my body works the way it's supposed to anymore, even though it might look like I'm perfectly fine." The knot of revelation tightened within her gut, a paralyzing fear momentarily stalling her tongue. When he started to move toward her, she rushed to finish. "It took me another three years just to learn how to walk independently and I have horrible scars. Dozens of them." She turned, so she wouldn't have to read the truth register in his eyes, and swallowed hard.

"It doesn't—"

"I never thought I'd see you again," she blurted, unwilling to hear the sympathy in his voice. "I knew you were in Europe, making your millions, achieving your dreams. I never thought you'd know, or that it would even matter. But then you came to New York, to the auction, and I told myself that being with you—even if it was only for a little while—was worth the risk. I knew you hated me. Knew you wanted to hurt me. But still, I rationalized that if I could hide the truth from you and be with you just once, I could create one last good memory of us. Together. I could finally know what I'd waited a lifetime to know, even if it meant losing you all over again."

His hand came to rest on her shoulder and she lurched sideways, away from the burning heat of his touch.

"But I was wrong. After we made love and I realized how I still felt about you, I knew the danger was too great." She struggled for breath, swallowing fiercely. "But you wouldn't stay away, would you? You convinced me, with your words and your mouth and your hands. I told myself I could handle your rejection and your hatred. I thought I could keep myself safe. But it was a lie."

"I don't hate you."

"I thought I could do it. I really thought I could. But your pity? Your disgust? Here, in the only place I've ever been truly happy?" She twisted her hands against her cramping stomach, the certainty of his response already tightening her chest and throat. "I'm sorry, but I can't."

The intensity in his eyes scalded her as he shook his head, reaching for her.

Scared of what would happen if he touched her again, she jerked backward, avoiding him. "You make me forget the risks. When you kiss me, it's too easy to delude myself into believing I can handle the pain…" She hesitated, her heart thudding wildly. "But I…" Fear crowded her chest, closing in on her hitching breaths. "I can't bear to see your reaction, to watch your desire turn to pity…"

Ethan reached for her again, his eyes flashing with stony resolve, and this time he moved too fast for her to escape him. Swiftly, Cate flung her hands between them, gripping his wrists to hold him at bay. "Don't!"

The muscles beneath her fingers turned to granite, his shuttered expression concealing his thoughts.

"Please don't," she whispered. "I know you want new memories and I know you feel like I owe you…but I can't." Tears scalded the backs of her eyes. "It hurts too much."

He processed her words for a moment in silence, then slowly twisted his forearms until her fingers could no longer hold him. She fought a wave of fear, swallowing against the salty tears that gathered in her throat. He pressed her hands down, anchoring them against her thighs, then stepped close enough to brush his chest against hers. She felt herself blanch, then redden, her body flushed with fear and worry and wanting.

"You think I pity you? That I'll turn from you in disgust?"

She nodded clumsily, biting the insides of her cheeks while he backed her against the side of her white bed. Anxiety dampened her face and neck, cooling her heated skin.

Ethan exhaled, one hand rising to align with her jaw. He tipped her face and waited. "Look at me."

When she finally did, she saw that her confession seemed to have solidified the layer of icy anger within his blue gaze. Where she'd expected only pity, disgust and rejection, she read banked fury and heated rage. He leaned down until his face hovered mere inches from her own. "Do you honestly think

I'm so shallow that I would desire you less simply because of a few scars?"

Trembling, she closed her eyes and pressed her lips hard against the urge to cry. "You haven't seen them."

"Then show me."

"No!"

"Yes." Reaching for her hips, he pressed his thumbs against the twin ridges of misaligned bone. Her body jerked and his hands went still. "Does that hurt?"

She shook her head miserably. As much as she wanted to lie to him, she couldn't. Not anymore.

"Show me."

Her skin burned beneath her dress while perspiration collected on her hands and upper lip. "I can't, Ethan...please don't...." The sweet torture of his hands against her damaged body was more than she could bear. But she didn't know how to fight him. How could she, when he was all her heart had ever wanted? Miserable and scared, she remained stiff and upright as he slowly pulled her close and bowed over her shoulders, splaying both hands over her back.

"I'm sorry you had to go through it alone," he breathed, his fingers warming her through the rumpled velvet of her dress. "I wish I'd been there for you."

The urge to weep surged anew within Cate's throat, but she swallowed hard to keep it contained. "I wanted you to be," she mumbled against his curved shoulder. "Apparently, when I was out of my mind with painkillers, I talked to you. Mrs. Bartholomew told me I begged you to come back. I even, on occasion when the pain was too much, dreamed you held me. They told me it was the drugs talking."

He lifted his head, his lungs working in ragged, unsteady pulls. Slowly, his hands resumed their circuit from shoulder to waist and back again. "So this is why you didn't want to be with me," he said in a low voice. "This is why you pushed me away."

She dipped her chin in a single, curt nod.

"You don't have to hide from me. Ever." Ethan leaned to kiss her with soft, satiny caresses of lip and breath that skimmed her brow, her cheek and the corner of her mouth. She stiffened when he reached for the zipper beneath her left arm, but forced herself to remain still as his fingers moved inexorably from rib to hip. The costume unfurled like the casing of a ripened fruit and tumbled to the floor, a tent of boned blue velvet against the beige sisal rug.

A hot blush fired her chest, contracting her nipples into hard points beneath the constricting white lace of her bustier bra. His fingers returned to her breasts and soon, her bra joined her corset on the floor. He pulled back to look at her, his eyes glittering as he explored her bared chest. "You'll always be beautiful to me, Cate. Always."

Shivers rode her skin as she stood half-naked before him, and the sheer force of her will kept her arms at her sides.

His eyes never left hers as he lifted his hands to trail along her rib cage, his fingers exploring the quivering tightness just beneath the final rung of bone. He then proceeded to unfasten the clasp of her skirt, lowering the zipper with a soft, snicking rasp. She swallowed repeatedly, shifting her weight clumsily as he lifted first one leg and then the other to divest her of skirt, panties and hose. He brushed her hip bones with his knuckles and then moved farther north, skimming her abdomen, her ribs and her inner arms.

She felt faint when he leaned to whisper soft, indecipherable nothings against her temple and his hands drifted up and back to her tense shoulder blades. She gripped his shirt and closed her eyes, unable to feign strength when he wandered perilously close to her damaged flesh. Holding her breath, she dipped her forehead against the knobby knuckles of her thumbs and waited, apprehension mounting behind her closed eyelids. With gentle tenderness and unexpected mercy, he skirted her naked back in favor of her hair. Threading his fingers through the slippery strands, he shook the cool length down her spine.

She shuddered, grateful for the temporary reprieve. His fingers skimmed her downturned jaw, then Ethan tipped her face up and aligned his lips with hers. He feasted on her mouth with a deep kiss that made her tremble. Made her want to weep. Her nipples grazed his crisp cotton tuxedo shirt while he adjusted the fit of their mouths. The fit of their bodies.

Her lips parted to welcome his demanding tongue, and he took advantage of her acquiescence, sealing her mouth with a dizzying combination of heat, moisture and drugging suction. He drove his tongue deep, delving the warm depths and dancing an intoxicating rhythm against her tender flesh.

She whimpered when his free hand dropped to chart the length of her spine. The ridges of her scars burned beneath his touch and he murmured soothing sounds into her mouth before detouring to the rounded shape of her buttocks and left thigh. Gripping her hip, he nudged her backward and up, stopping only when she felt the rigid swell of his erection tightly contained within his pants. He rocked against her, forcing her to acknowledge his burning eagerness to join with her.

A small sob caught against her throat and she ripped her mouth aside, gasping for breath. Giving her no time to retreat, he lifted her until she tipped above his hand, one knee cocked high against his hip while her buttocks pressed securely against the edge of her bed. Grappling for balance, she looped her arms over his shoulders and closed her eyes as his fingers slowly parted her, stroking the intimate flesh.

Cate trembled involuntarily as he slid one long finger inside her, a low moan escaping her lips. He bent to reclaim her mouth, quieting her with another kiss. Helpless within his arms, she undulated against him until he answered the demand of her body with a second, then a third finger. *Yes*, she breathed silently, hard shudders of pleasure mounting. *More.* She wanted Ethan with every cell of her body. She wanted to feel him everywhere. Inside, outside, until all the empty spaces were filled. Until she felt whole again.

He lifted her until both her legs clamped around his waist, fitting the ridge of his clothed erection against the damp notch above his fingers. Slowly, the delicious friction heated her sensitive flesh. The pleasure built, driving higher, intensifying until the lazy, unfaltering rhythm became too much. She felt herself tightening, throbbing, reaching for that bright moment of release. His lips claimed hers again, his tongue mimicking the motion of his fingers and hips, flooding her with a poignant ache. Oh, Ethan… *"Ethan!"*

"Shh." Ethan lifted his head and his fingers slid free just as the rocketing longing neared its peak. "Hold on," he whispered while she trembled against him.

"I can't," she managed, her breath coming out in thin, thready filaments of need.

His finger mapped the taut line of her jaw. "You can. I'm going to keep you on the edge until you accept how much I want you. Still. No scar can ever change that." Ethan lowered her to her feet and then slowly turned her stomach toward the mattress before gently pushing her shoulders toward the bed.

"Oh, Ethan, please don't," she said, twisting miserably in an attempt to block his view of her mutilated back.

He ignored her protests, catching her flailing arms and pulling them taut until she lay stretched out before him. With one quick shift of his hands, he manacled both wrists between his fingers and thumb. Still clothed, he dragged his free palm over her bared back, skimming the rigid bumps and quivering valleys of her scars while humiliation scalded her lungs.

It was the worst place he could have touched her, smoothing his warm palm along the most damaged part of her body, the part that kept her from feeling like a true woman. Icy dread flooded her, and she buried her burning eyes into the unforgiving mattress so she wouldn't see revulsion mar his beautiful features. "Ethan," she moaned, as the insistent heat of his fingers continued to press and probe, drawing shivers from her sensitive flesh. "You don't have to—"

"Stop talking," he said gently, then he dipped his head to silence any additional complaints. Warm lips pressed against the base of her spine and then slowly moved higher, nuzzling her wounded flesh in tender, coaxing acceptance. His mouth and tongue touched each sensitized track of pain left behind by her surgeries, stroking and petting her as her insecurities gathered and crested. "You're beautiful," he murmured against her nape before reaching to rub the swell of her buttocks in small, soothing circles. A thumb drifted up to press against one of the twin dimples at her lower back, then he dropped his forehead to rest quietly against her crooked vertebrae. "All of you, whether it's scarred or not," he breathed.

When a whimper formed her only response, he gently rolled her to her back and ordered her to open her eyes. A violent blush scalded her chest as she miserably shook her head and covered her face with her hands.

"Look at me," he insisted, forcing her palms away from her cheeks. When she finally acquiesced, he stepped from between her thighs and tore at his clothing until he stood before her, naked and rampantly aroused. "Does it look like I want you any less than I did before?"

Wordlessly, she shook her head, her throat thickening with unshed tears.

"I'll always want you, Catydid. No matter what." Tenderness softened his features as he bent between her knees and then spread her thighs wide with his hot, commanding palms. "Always."

Biting back her moan, she relaxed her legs and arched her weeping center toward his mouth. White light claimed her vision as she felt his hair brush her inner thighs, then spun into colors as he dragged his tongue along her exposed skin. Small, nibbling kisses teased her, then became greedy as he probed deeper. He sucked, long, dragging pulls against the musk-scented opening of her body while her senses narrowed to heavy, thudding awareness of his mouth against her flesh. Again, she neared the flashpoint of rapture, pleasure and aching pain mingling as she teetered precariously at the edge. He drew back slightly and blew a cool, teasing exhalation against her abraded sex, then dipped to toy with her again.

Excruciating, exquisitely light strokes made electricity surge along her thighs, behind her eyelids and deep within her core. She arched toward his mouth, lifting, pressing and begging him with ragged, panting sounds.

When she thought she could bear no more, he withdrew again. "I want you," he repeated. With his gaze locked on hers, he straightened to stand naked before her. A tightly muscled chest, covered with a smattering of crisp black hair, and his long, knotted arms bore mute testimony to his tempered strength. "Tell me you believe me."

Unwilling to lie, she hid behind an upflung arm.

Stepping close again, Ethan slid his palms beneath her buttocks and tipped her tender flesh toward him. Her breath hitched as she adjusted to the sensation of his skin against hers. "Tell me."

She squirmed to bring him closer, hooking a leg around his buttocks and tugging hard.

Still, he resisted, drawing out the torture of their almost-joining until she whimpered.

"Look at me."

She opened her eyes to find him staring at her with focused intensity. His hard, lean limbs, damp with sweat, the startling width of his shoulders and chest and all the lovely places where hair-roughened skin stretched over hot, twitching muscle brought a swell of emotion to her chest.

"Tell me, Cate."

She lifted shaking fingers to the tight muscles of his abdomen. How could this beautiful man still want her? How? Tears blurred her eyes and her breath escaped in a great, shuddering rush. "I believe you."

Thick lashes fanned against his cheek and he bent to press his forehead to hers. "Thank God," he answered on a gruff exhalation. He surged forward, pushing her back on the bed and then joining her there, his knees pressing her thighs wide. Leaning down, he caught her mouth with his while his hand lowered to guide himself inside her.

Delicious pleasure rocketed through Cate as he filled her, sliding deep until they aligned, hip to hip and groin to groin. They gasped in mutual pleasure as the contrast of soft against hard, of driving pressure against yielding acceptance, formed an achingly sweet union of their flesh.

Cate dragged her hands down Ethan's back, the taut muscles flexing beneath her fingers, while he clutched her hips, holding her fast as he pounded into her with savage, rhythmic thrusts. "Don't doubt me again," he told her between ragged breaths.

She trembled greedily against each slick, powerful lunge, and whispered against his demanding mouth. "No."

Ethan's eyes glittered with emotion. "I've never stopped wanting you…ever." A moan rumbled in his chest as he stiffened, the rush of release pushing them both toward the peak.

And then they reached it. Tumbled over the edge.

Afterward, pressed snugly beneath his sweat-slicked chest, desire and longing and relief twisted into a knot of emotion too big for Cate to contain. Try as she might, she couldn't stem the tide that swept through her, a bright, shimmering wave of emotion so fierce she could scarcely breathe.

Unable to contain the rush of feeling, it spilled over into tears, taking all of her defenses with it. Her chest ached. Her throat hurt. And she felt exposed. Raw. Vulnerable. Her lungs burned with the intensity of it.

Gasping, her eyes brimmed anew as wet, sloppy tracks of tears channeled down her temples and into her ears. Distressed by her lack of control, she dug her face into his chest and tried to hide. Messy and noisy, embarrassed and bereft, she fought in vain to silence her great, gulping sobs.

"Cate." His voice, strung tight, plucked against her heart while he started to withdraw from her.

"Don't go!" she blurted, pulling him back with legs, arms, hands and feet. "Don't!"

"I'm not going anywhere," he soothed as he settled back against her and then rolled them both onto their sides. She felt his hard, unyielding body against hers while one wide hand smoothed her hair back from her face.

Too overwhelmed to thank him aloud, she merely nodded while shuddering sobs racked her ribs. Hot tears leaked down her cheeks, and she couldn't stop them, no matter how hard she tried. She couldn't. And her vulnerability terrified her.

She'd kept everything inside for so long, kept her heart and her emotions and her pain walled off from the world, that now that the dam had broken, there was nothing she could do to repair it.

"Hey," he said, rubbing one hand over her quivering belly. He reached her hip and rolled her onto her side against him, murmuring an anguished plea against her hair. "Did I do something wrong?" he asked.

She mumbled a tortured no.

"Then what?"

How to explain? He'd been as wonderful as he'd always been, despite all the awful things she'd done to him, despite the wretched condition of her damaged body. She didn't know how to defend herself against the onslaught of feelings he invoked. "I'm sorry," she gulped, the words wrenching out in a distressed moan. "I don't know why I'm crying like this."

"It's okay," he crooned, pulling her even closer. Warm fingers trailed down her back, navigating the bumps and scars along her spine as he slowly rocked her against his chest. He held her as she wept, until she felt wrung out and empty. When she sniffed and swiped a wrist below her swollen eyes, he cupped his hand over her damp nape and whispered, "It'll be all right, Cate. I promise I'll make it all right."

She believed him. Despite all her fears, despite her doubts, she knew that with Ethan, she would be safe. So she nodded jerkily and hauled in a hiccupping breath. Lifting her tear-streaked face, she leaned to press her mouth to his throat. "I know," she said. "But will you convince me again?"

He obliged her without preamble, taking her lips in a long, sweeping kiss. His tongue gently abraded hers, sending delicious tremors through her limbs. With infinite skill, he probed and caressed and stroked until her tears dried and her mind reeled. Dizzying, languid pleasure seeped through her, the responsive ache collecting deep within, echoing against her hip, where he'd become hard again. Sighing, she arched against him and pulled him closer. Together, they rolled, her calf hooked around him and his weight settling atop her.

A low moan escaped her throat as she felt him adjust her pelvis and then enter her, until she had accommodated every inch of his length. She lifted her hips and her eyelids fluttered closed, trying to draw him closer while a consuming hunger ate its way through her flesh. Her breath hitched, hung, then rushed out in a grand rush as he slowly withdrew and then lowered against her again. Harder this time. Deeper as her body welcomed him.

Their twined fingers moved to her hips as he lifted and pulled her against him. Again and again, she writhed to seat him farther inside. The sweet craving for release increased sharply, gaining momentum with each advance and retreat. Every delicious lunge, thickening and hardening within the channel of her body, intensified the pleasure until she could contain the rapture no longer.

Convulsing against him, she arched uncontrollably while his name tore from her lips. Ethan silenced her pleas with a low growl, his mouth claiming and containing hers until his own release ripped a raw grunt from deep within his chest. He pulsed violently against her quivering flesh, his thighs flexing hard atop her limp limbs.

Spent, they remained fused together for an endless, breathless moment, their bodies clinging intimately. Cate didn't want to move ever again. Her eyelids felt weighted, too heavy to lift. A protest hummed in her throat when she felt him ease sideways onto the bed, his softening length slipping free as he adjusted her legs and tucked her body against his.

"Better?" he mumbled groggily, his grip on her waist slackening.

Nodding wordlessly against his chest, she listened to the steady thudding of his heart as he drifted off to sleep. Clutching his broad rib cage, she realized Ethan had claimed more than just her pride and her virginity and her secrets. He'd claimed everything. Her trust, her hopes and her dreams for a future that could never be. She'd surrendered them all to him.

CHAPTER THIRTEEN

CATE awoke to find afternoon's light slanting across her bed and floor. It took less than half a second for her to remember that she wasn't alone, and one additional beat of breath for her to feel the heat of Ethan's gaze upon her profile. Knowing that the beautiful, virile man of her dreams now lay beside her, sated from their lovemaking and watching her, sent a flutter of nervous awareness through her belly.

He made her feel beautiful again. And for a moment, watching him bask in the slanted afternoon sun, she could almost believe that it would be enough. She could almost believe that her other scars, those buried too deep to see, wouldn't matter.

But she'd be wrong.

Don't borrow trouble, she heard Mrs. Bartholomew's voice say. *Just take it one day at a time.*

There'd be time enough for second thoughts tomorrow.

Today, she'd live for the moment. She'd steep herself in Ethan and collect beautiful memories for the bleak, lonely days ahead. She'd savor the time she had with him before reality came crashing back. Before they both remembered the reasons things could never work between them.

So she eased back to look at him, propping her head upon her upturned hand. Rumpled from sleep and with the warm yellow light softening the harsh planes of his face, Ethan looked like some pagan god brought to life. Like the boy she'd fallen in love with so long ago.

He looked impossibly young. Accepting and open. And beautifully, wonderfully naked. Cate's eyes drifted back to his. They glinted with amused blue fire, framed by a thick fan of lashes. Black stubble cast shadows on his jaw and neck, and he'd canted up on one elbow to watch her, his chin resting indolently against his palm. The long bulge of his biceps merged with the swell of deltoid and shoulder, giving way to the slope of his neck and the dent of sternum sprinkled with black, curling hair.

Tentatively, she reached to brush her fingertip along the ridge of sinew below his wrist. Her touch turned featherlight as she traced the faint blue line of vein to his palm, to his chin, down to the knot of masculinity in his throat, then farther south to the springy thatch of hair on his chest.

He remained utterly still as she ventured farther, his breath suspended as her fingers drew nearer to the impressive ridge of arousal heating the space between them.

His eyes darkened to cobalt when she reached her destination, a low hiss of breath escaping his throat when she flattened her palm against his hardness.

Before she'd even had time to realize what was happening, he'd flipped her over and pinned her beneath him. Their combined weight pressed her deep into the mattress, making her feel deliciously overpowered. Deliciously dizzy and aroused.

"Careful, Catydid." Just hearing his voice, deep and tender, awakened places deep within, tuning her inner chords to the melody he'd written for the two of them so long ago.

"Or what?" she teased, reaching to stroke her fingers through the hair falling over his eyes.

He stared at her without answering, his nostrils flaring and the cadence of his breathing picking up speed. Her breasts, tender and aching already, yearned for the heavy press of his chest. Anticipation gathered in her veins, turning to liquid fire as he settled his weight between her thighs. Spreading her legs wide, she tipped to meet him, hard against soft, as his hips nestled close within the cradle of hers. Pleasure shot through her and she felt her nipples harden. Seeing the yearning, reaching tips, he dropped to trail damp, teasing nibbles between her breasts. Then he shifted left and pulled her straining nipple into his hot, hot mouth.

She arched against him with a gasp, a moan gathering volume within her throat. But then she felt his tongue move against her flesh and lost all focus as his ministrations brought an acute edge of need to her arousal. When he switched his attentions to her other breast, she writhed against him, urging him closer with hands and fingers and hips. And still he tarried, licking and sucking and teasing while sensation coiled sharply, hot and unbearably sweet within her veins. Hungry, wanting and blinded by desire, she rocked her pelvis against his.

"Look at me," he said, pulling free of her breast and bracing himself above her. "I want to watch you when you—"

"Not without you," she panted, reaching for his neck as she rocked against him again. And again. Fanning the flames between them as her pleasure skirted the boundaries of pain.

"Do you know how much I've dreamed of this?" His eyes glittered and he reached to press his forehead against hers. "Every day and every damned night, I dreamed of this. Of you." He moved within her again until she thought she could stand no more of the sweet torture without coming apart.

Her mouth dropped open and his name rode her pleading exhale.

Hearing her, he stopped for a moment and remained still, the undeniable perfection of their fit bringing tears to her eyes. "This is what I've wanted, Cate. Always."

Desperate to show her agreement, she arched up to kiss him. And in that rough union of their mouths, she realized it didn't matter what he did or didn't say. She was lost. Mindless now, she rocked with him, her craving for release blinding her to all else. Heated pleasure coiled high, spreading through her limbs and sparking light on the periphery of her vision. She was close. So, so close.

"Tell me," he urged, the muscles in his back rigid beneath her palms. "Tell me what you want."

She whimpered, hovering at the brink and unable to find the words.

"I…" she managed. "Just don't…oh…"

"Like this?"

She bucked beneath him, arching her head against the mattress while both hands clutched against his ribs. *Yes. Yes. Like this.*

Her final thread of coherence drew taut and then snapped. Her climax gripped her, lifting her hips from the bed and vaulting her into a storm of crashing pleasure. The spasms went on and on and on, clamping hard while he thickened even more within her. When the last shuddering wave of release rippled through her quivering limbs, he dipped to kiss her, a gentle grazing of his lips.

"Good?" he murmured.

Tears gathered and she nodded, reaching to pull him close. Being with Ethan, here, like this, felt right. Like home. She was meant for this. Meant for him. And she'd be his for as long as he'd allow it.

After a moment, he resumed his rhythmic strokes. She relaxed beneath him, welcomed the weight of his body atop hers, and ran encouraging hands against the bunched muscles of his shoulders and upper arms. Soon, his own drive for pleasure overtook gentleness, and the wet, rhythmic sounds of their erotic mating filled the room.

He groaned, shifting onto his knees and reaching to lift her buttocks up onto his thighs. Strong hands positioned her while ropy tendons stood out on his neck and his chest worked like bellows with his breath. When he'd seated himself as deep as their position would allow, he gripped her buttocks and tilted her even higher, driving into her in rough, blind pursuit of his own release.

She'd never watched anything so beautiful. Knowing that she could provoke such passion in him suffused her with joy. No matter what happened tomorrow, she knew that now, right now, she was his world. And she reveled in it.

He roared and shoved deep one more time, his muscles turning to stone beneath her hands. For one breathless, shuddering moment, he swayed above her, caught in the throes of his orgasm. And then he collapsed atop her, murmuring her name in an odd combination of gratitude and exhaustion.

Smiling, she reached to lift the damp hair from his nape. "Good?" she murmured with a grin.

He rolled to her side and gathered her close, leaning to press his lips against her forehead. "With you? Always."

She burrowed close, savoring the contrast of texture and the hint of musk that clung to their flesh. "I think I like you better naked," she told him. "You're not nearly so fierce without your clothes on."

He growled, rolling to trap her between his thighs. "You wouldn't want me gentle."

True. Rather than answer, she squirmed free, clambering to her knees and shoving the hair out of her eyes. "Race you to the beach," she challenged him before launching from the bed.

He lunged for her, catching the notch of her waist and hauling her back onto the mattress while she squealed. Pinning her beneath one long leg, he tapped the tip of her nose with one finger. "Not so fast," he warned. "I'll race you. But when

I win, you'll pay *my* forfeit, Catydid, and it sure as hell won't be shells."

She blinked innocently, enjoying her capture enough to not care who won. "Deal."

Five minutes later, Ethan had already reached the edge of the water. Dressed in blue swimming trunks and nothing else, he dove into the cool, clear water and embraced the transition from hot white sand to the soothing kiss of the sea. Treading water, he turned to stare back toward the beach house, wondering what was keeping Cate. It wasn't like her to lose. Ever. Especially when the competition occurred anywhere near the beach.

His beach.

He smiled, realizing that he'd experienced more pleasure in the past five hours than he'd had in the nine years he'd worked here as a boy. Remembering the way he'd spent himself in Cate and the way she'd responded beneath him, he felt himself harden despite the cold water.

He scanned the walkway, caught sight of Cate and then froze, losing his bearings entirely when a rogue wave caught him and sent him under. When he emerged, it was to find Cate grinning at him, her silhouette framed by blinding sun and blue, blue sky. "Swim much?" she teased.

"You…" Words failed him as he flung water from his hair and devoured her with his eyes. "You lost."

"Your bikini choice slowed me down." Cocking a brow, she indicated the scraps of triangular fabric he'd chosen as her suit. "I feel practically naked in this getup, and it took forever to figure out how to tie the pieces together."

Ethan battled a second surge of lust as he looked at her. Three green-and-pink flowered triangles, strung precariously together with ribbon and loops of metal drew his gaze and wouldn't let go. A low growl clamored for release as he scanned her groomed toes, her long, slim legs, the curve of her waist and the lovely, tempting swell of her breasts. She'd donned sunglasses that shaded her eyes and tied her blond hair back in some haphazard knot that just begged his fingers to take it down.

He waded through the water to the sand and then strode toward her, drawing close while a blush tinted her chest and neck. With her hand shading her eyes, she tipped her head back to maintain eye contact. She smelled like sunscreen and tropical flowers, a heady combination that tempted him to haul her back into her scented room and make love to her until night fell. Until they both grew old and wrinkled and couldn't see anymore.

Too late, he realized the path his thoughts had taken. He felt as if he'd been hit by yet another wave, fighting the realization that pebbled his skin. Since when had he started thinking of sex as making love? Since when had wanting her in his bed changed to wanting her in his life?

"How's the water?" she asked, curling those pink toenails into the wet sand.

"It's great," he mumbled as he stared at her, his breath pummeling his chest. "You'll like it."

"Are you sure?" she asked. Her hand, warm against his wet flesh, alit upon his arm. "It's not too cold?"

Shaken, his thoughts reeling, he dipped his gaze to her slim fingers. And suddenly, he realized he didn't care about his revenge anymore. Cate didn't deserve to be punished. She deserved to be loved. By him. Perhaps she always had.

Oh, God.

A sick sense of dread washed over him as his thoughts turned to the avalanche of disaster he'd already set into motion. It had required quick footwork and countless calls, but the players were all engaged now. The contracts were drawn up and signed. The train wreck he'd sent into motion already had wheels and fuel. Within ten days, Cate's company would be reduced to mere scraps, its healthy components sold out from under her and its real estate rented out to the highest bidder.

Could he stop it?

Or was it too late?

"Welcome home, dear," said Mrs. Bartholomew the Monday after Cate returned home from the island. "How was work?"

"Long." Cate sighed, shrugged off her coat, then hung it in the front entryway closet. Concentrating on the daily grind of business when she hadn't heard from Ethan since their flight home had definitely taken its toll.

Not that she expected him to call. Despite their idyllic day and endless night on the island, she knew he wasn't the type to drag things out once they'd ended. He'd been very clear about his opinion regarding relationships. He believed in physical pleasure and no emotional messiness. No love.

Besides, she couldn't offer what he needed anyway. He needed someone healthy, someone strong. Someone who didn't have to visit doctors every few months because her body didn't work right anymore. Heartsick, exhausted and fighting a ridiculous welling of tears, she mustered a smile. "If it's all right with you, I think I'll just take a hot bath and turn in early tonight."

"You might want to visit the study first."

The study was the *last* place she wanted to go. "Can't it wait until the morning?"

"I don't think so, dear. Ethan's been waiting over an hour already."

"Ethan?" Anticipation and hope surged as Cate darted down the hall. She flung the door open and then froze, struck immobile by surprise.

Vase upon vase of flowers crowded the desktop, filling her

vision with every tropical hue: riotous pinks, blinding yellows, deep reds, scandalous purples and rich creams. Their scent filled the room, steeping her senses in memories of the island and startling her heart into a frenzy of thudding beats.

"Did you miss me?" Ethan asked from the shadows. The way he murmured the question, an intoxicating blend of warmth and lust, made her wonder how she'd ever thought to keep herself from loving him. As much as she knew she shouldn't, as hard as she'd tried to keep her heart safe, she loved him.

"Very much," she whispered.

"Show me." He sat sprawled on the couch, beckoning her forward with a beguiling smile. "Come. Sit."

A dizzying hope pulsed beneath the surface of her skin, making her tremble as she moved to perch beside him on the wide leather couch. He twirled a single orchid between his thumb and forefinger, and as she watched, he leaned to brush its plump petals along her cheek. The lavish perfume and decadent softness brought a stinging bite of tears to the back of her throat.

"I haven't been able to stop thinking of you," he breathed, canting his head and claiming her mouth in a drugging kiss.

For a moment, she lost herself in the magic of his lips against hers, the warm, heady pulse of arousal banishing her earlier fatigue.

"Did you think about me?" he asked against the sensitive patch of skin beneath her ear.

"I thought we'd concluded our transactions," she gasped, arching her neck to grant him better access. "No messy emotional entanglements, remember?"

"I was wrong," he murmured. "I want to get messy with you."

Much, much later, rumpled and happy and so much in love

her heart didn't seem to fit properly in her chest, Cate kissed Ethan goodbye with a promise of tomorrow hovering on his lips.

She returned to the study to find a blown glass bowl and an oblong envelope nestled among the vases of flowers. The large bowl had been filled with countless pink and white shells of various shapes and sizes and etched along its scalloped edge, the words *I will pay whatever forfeit you ask and it will still never be enough* snapped her love for him into even sharper focus.

Cupping a palm over her mouth, she tried to contain the trembling that overtook the muscles of her face. Dare she hope? Dare she dream of a future she'd never thought possible?

Gathering up the envelope, she ran a trembling thumb beneath its seal. Inside, she found a heavy sheet of cream paper, this one folded in thirds. Shaking it out, she saw that it was filled with Ethan's bold, slanted scrawl.

My dearest Catydid,
I am yours. Always.
No matter what happens, remember that.
E

Cate inhaled sharply and refolded the paper, pressing the letter between her palms and biting her quivering lips to keep from bursting into tears.

I am yours, too, Ethan. I always have been.

CHAPTER FOURTEEN

Nine days of bliss later, Cate stood at her office windows in the Carrington Building, staring sightlessly at the spattered raindrops on the wide wall of glass. Despite it being closer to noon, the overcast skies and persistent rain made it feel like it was far later. The weather matched her mood perfectly, and she lifted a palm to the cold glass. A thin mist of fog gathered around her flattened fingertips, then swiftly dissipated as her hand cooled.

Behind her, strewn across her desk and filled with far too many lines of damning truth, lay the most recent report from Joe Benson. Not wishing to alarm her until he'd known for sure, her father's most trusted advisor had assigned four different teams from two different firms to research the previous two weeks' stock transactions. This morning, a mere three hours and eight minutes after she'd climbed from Ethan's warm bed, Joe had provided copies of everything: the contracts that had been drawn up without her knowledge; the records of dissolution for multiple small enterprises Carrington Industries had funded; the votes that had been cast during the only board meeting she'd missed since her father's death. With the evidence too convincing to deny, she'd been forced to acknowledge the truth.

She no longer controlled her own company.

And by tomorrow morning, her father's company, the

company that had been in the Carrington family for over a century, would cease to exist. The Manhattan headquarters, the seat of Carrington Industries for nearly as long, was being subdivided and rented out to competing companies. The family's properties, its businesses, its charities…all of it. Gone. Dismantled. Destroyed or sold or absorbed into one of Ethan's subsidiaries.

And she hadn't suspected a thing.

With her throat too dry to swallow, Cate opened her mouth and dragged in a steadying breath. How had this happened? How had she not seen it?

Because she'd seen only what Ethan allowed her to see. And she'd wanted to believe in him. In the two of them. She'd wanted to be loved so, so much.

But she'd been wrong. Stupid and blind and wrong. The whole time he'd been seducing her, breaking down her defenses and making her fall in love with him again, he'd been plotting against her. Hating her. Biding his time until he could destroy her.

Shock coursed through her, lacerating her chest, her heart, her lungs. Cate willed her brain to keep thinking despite the pain. Oh, God. It hurt. Worse than she'd ever imagined.

Closing her eyes, she berated herself for not heeding her own warnings. She should have trusted her first instincts. She'd known he hated her, known he wanted revenge. What she hadn't known was how far he'd go to hurt her. Taking her virginity wasn't enough. Pretending to accept her scars and making her believe in love again wasn't enough. No. He had to destroy every facet of her life. Her heart. Her company. Her memories.

Her lungs tightened. Seized. Grew sluggish with cold, icy pain. How he must have laughed at her pitiful weaknesses and flaws. How he must have gloated once he'd reached her vulnerable core. And still, confident that his secrets remained undiscovered, he continued to lie. He systematically tightened the web he'd spun around her, pulling her closer and closer while he orchestrated her demise behind the scenes.

Painful cramps wrenched her empty stomach. Her throat burned. Her legs quaked. Too shocked to cry, she could only stare blindly down at the empty parking lot. How much longer had he planned to continue the ruse? How many more times had he planned to make love to her, to murmur endearments against her flesh while he seduced her into compliance?

Her chest tightened, struggled to draw breath while her lips worked soundlessly. She couldn't bear it. Couldn't bear that she loved him when everything he'd said, everything he'd done, was a lie. Pressing her knuckles against her mouth, she dropped her forehead to the glass while uncontrollable tremors claimed her limbs.

A slight knock gifted her with a shred of strength, and she straightened. Before the door even opened, Cate felt a prickling warmth steal over her skin, inching its way from her fingertips to her hairline. Trapped, she turned and tried to affect a calm demeanor. The numbness that had clogged her limbs since reading the lawyers' reports turned to tingling needles of ice. The door opened and her assistant ushered Ethan in with a cheerful smile and a promise to fetch fresh coffee.

He assured her it wasn't necessary and then closed the door with a soft, ominous click.

Unwelcome desire, laced with thawing anger and wrenching pain, rose to flutter against her ribs.

"Hello, gorgeous."

The deep voice sent her senses off kilter, spinning her world off its axis. Could she pretend she didn't know? She tried to affix a pleasant smile to her face, failed miserably in the attempt, then ducked her head to disguise her unease. "I didn't expect you so soon."

He walked toward her while her thoughts careened like a wild carnival ride. It amazed her that she could feel such a consuming blend of anger, betrayal and need for another person, that having him near sent her heart into such a clumsy, thudding delirium. She had trouble breathing normally, and it required scrupulous effort to appear serene.

"I missed you," he said, crossing the muffling carpet and joining her at the window. "What do you say we have lunch together?"

Cate lifted her eyes while her nerves stretched taut. *What do I say to him?* Unlike two weeks ago, when the distrustful gleam in his gaze testified to the shield he'd erected between them and warned her to keep her distance, he'd perfected a look of open, unfettered yearning.

Now, with less than two weeks of practice, he looked as if he truly meant all the things he'd whispered against her damp flesh. Gone was the thinly veiled hatred in his expression. Gone was the sardonic twist to his mouth, the shuttered inscrutability within his eyes.

With his hard, embittered edge buried too deep to see, his magnetism increased exponentially. She felt herself drawing closer. Yielding. Wanting to believe in him, despite the damning truth.

But she couldn't succumb to her insatiable longing for him. She mustn't. She'd made her mistakes. But she'd never deliberately hurt him just because she could. She didn't deserve this, no matter what she'd done. So she simply stood silent and still, her throat working with her labored breaths, until his fingers lifted, oh so gently, and the pad of his thumb came to rest on the crest of her cheek.

"You okay?" he asked. His thumb grazed her skin as if he were testing the satiny marble polish of a museum sculpture, too precious to treat with anything less than reverence and awe.

She stepped sideways, anything to preserve her resolve,

but he caught her easily. Inexorably, he drew her closer, until her knees bumped his legs.

"Hey," he said, jostling the side of her neck with one hand.

Unable to meet his eyes, she kept her face tipped down. Undeterred, he slowly brought her into the cove of his arms, aligning their bodies until her forehead touched his sternum. The heady scent of his skin caught at her lungs, flooding her with an unwanted, blind hunger. She wanted him, for far more than the simple pleasure his touch elicited. She wanted him for the false feeling of completeness he wrought. She wanted the happiness she'd foolishly believed he could provide.

She wanted him because she'd never, ever stopped loving him.

But the man she loved was a lie. A horrible, horrible lie.

Her scarred and damaged body didn't seem to care.

Though he'd done nothing more than press his wide, warm hands against her upper back and shoulders, she heated unbearably beneath his touch. Yearning leaked from her heart and lungs into the cells of her skin and bones. She felt his breath against her scalp and shivered, fighting the desire to be closer, to feel him against her skin, to lose herself in him once more. What she wouldn't give to join with him, to pretend she didn't know the truth.

What she wouldn't give to make love to the only man she'd ever wanted.

But she mustn't. She mustn't.

"You were right," she finally whispered after a long, long time.

"About what?" His lips stirred her hair.

"Me knowing you," she managed in a shaky voice. She withdrew enough to meet his eyes. "You really aren't the boy I once knew, are you?"

He went perfectly still, his breath suspended against her forehead.

"I know that now," she said quietly, stepping from his arms while the knot in her chest grew harder. Heavier. Threatening to swallow her with its oppressive blackness. "I know, Ethan."

His arms fell to his sides as his jaw flexed. He swallowed, silent.

"When were you planning to tell me?" she asked.

"I wasn't."

Lightning cracked, casting a blinding flash of blue highlights on Ethan's dense black locks. She resisted the urge to touch the silky strands and laced her fingers into a tight, bruising knot of thwarted dreams. "You thought I'd be so distracted, so in love with the man you're pretending to be, that I wouldn't notice?"

His eyes glittered as he stared at her and she could see his pulse thrumming beneath his jaw, echoing the throbbing cacophony within her own chest. "It's not what you think."

"Isn't it?"

His answer was a low, intimate murmur. "No."

Cate's gaze skipped from his to the strong line of his shadowed jaw while hot, black anger coiled in her chest. "Right. And I'm supposed to believe you."

A dull red flush stained his neck.

"Get out."

"Cate, I—"

"Get out!" She lifted her arm and pointed at the door, grateful for the rage that kept her arm steady and her legs strong.

For a long moment, Ethan stood without moving as silent tension spun between them. Cate stared at him, at the knotted fists at his sides and the ticking pulse beneath his jaw, and wondered how long she could remain upright without falling apart.

"No," he finally said. "I won't leave you again."

Her stomach bottomed out and her arm fell to her side.

"Why? Because you want to savor your victory?" A strangled bleat of disbelief caught in her throat. "Because you want to watch me bleed?"

"Because I need to explain," he said.

She shook her head, feeling oddly as if she were a witness to her own execution. He wanted to explain? "You think there's a way that I'll accept what you did? That some magic combination of words will make this...this horrid, wretched betrayal something other than it is?"

He swallowed and refused to drop his gaze. "Yes."

She wanted to pretend he had an explanation that would make everything better. But she was through deluding herself. Through with finding comfort in lies. "Fine." She'd listen. She'd let him say his piece, then she'd never have to see him again. "Explain."

"Thank you."

She backed away from his approach, putting her father's desk between them. Turning from him, she stared in silence out at the bruised purple clouds. Concentrating on the slanting rain, she prayed for a swift end to her torment.

Just make it fast.

Ethan stood two yards from her, stark and unmoving, and the silence between them grew heavy, as thick and toxic as smoke. She couldn't breathe. And yet silence was safer than speech. Safer than confronting his lies.

"I never meant for you to find out," he finally told her in a low, quiet voice.

"That doesn't help your case," she answered without meeting his eyes, "and before you spin me more lies, you need to know that I'm not going to change—"

"Just listen first," he interrupted, "and then you can tell me what you will and won't do."

She turned her gaze to his and found him staring at her, his blue eyes glittering from within the shadows of his lean face. Unable to maintain eye contact, she resumed her study of the clouds while her trepidation built.

He leaned toward her, his hands pressing flat against the incriminating papers strewn atop her desk. "I need to say some things to you, things I should have said two weeks ago."

"There's nothing you can say that will make up for what you've done."

"Damn it, Cate, I have to try." He hauled in a steadying breath, and waited until she turned her head to look at him. "You were right about the lies. And you were right about me hating you, wanting revenge. But I've changed. You changed me."

A dark pain threatened to overwhelm her. More lies—it was the one thing she couldn't bear. "You haven't."

"I know you don't believe me," he said gruffly. "But let me finish. Let me try to salvage our future."

She swallowed, the knot in her throat thickening enough to choke her. She had no future with Ethan. No future at all.

Ethan didn't move to touch her, though his eyes didn't release their claim on hers. He just leaned forward, bracing his elbows as he addressed her. "My soul was connected to yours before you even knew who I was." His gaze scanned her face, his black hair gleaming in the filtered light of her lamp. "Did you know that?"

She stared at him in silence.

"You were nine the first time I saw you, skinny and awkward and shining with some inner light that drew me like a moth to a flame. I couldn't have stayed away if I'd tried. Dad told me who you were, who your father was and warned me that you couldn't play with me. He said you were to be admired from a distance, like the pictures in a glossy magazine or an actor on television. But I couldn't keep my distance, no matter how wrong and impossible it was. I wanted to be near you. And we were young enough that you allowed it."

Her vision blurred as she recalled the earnest, careful boy he'd once been. Even then, she'd sensed his caution, had yearned to draw him out, to make him carefree and happy instead of so solemn and quiet.

"And the best part was, the differences between us didn't seem to matter. You didn't care that I didn't come from money. You didn't care that I didn't attend a fancy school or wear all the right clothes. You were my best friend, Cate, and I grew to love you more than I think any other man has loved a woman."

He stared at her as she blinked back the film of tears.

"For a long time after you sent me away, I tried to convince myself that what I felt back then was an illusion based on lies. That I hated you for toying with me, for pretending to love me when you didn't. But I was wrong. No matter how much I wished it otherwise, no matter how many other women I saw, I couldn't let go of you. And I don't want to fight it anymore."

"Then why?" she began, misery welling in her throat. "Why did you do this?"

"I told you I wanted to buy the island for my father, remember? I wanted to give him his pride back and I told myself that by giving him the island, the home where he'd lived for years as someone else's servant, it would help. He's spent his life believing he wasn't good enough, that we weren't good enough, and I've spent the last ten years trying to prove him wrong. But nothing ever works, you know? People believe what they're going to believe, and you can't change it. At least that's what I've always thought."

"Ethan—"

"But I was wrong, Cate. I was wrong about a lot of things. It turns out I've been lying to myself just as much as I've been lying to you. Yes, I bought the island for my father. But I also bought it for me. I never really moved past your rejection and I think that buying the island was a way for me to prove that your hold on me wasn't real, that it was just a carryover from my unrequited adolescent crush and the insecurities of my youth. I thought that if I owned the place you'd sent me away from, I could forget. Buying your island, pursuing you, hell, even making love to you that first time, it was just me trying to eliminate my obsession with all the things I'd been told I couldn't have, all the things I wasn't supposed to feel. But when you sent me away again, all those old feelings of inadequacy returned. It was like I was that poor, groveling kid again, trying to earn your love. And it hurt. It made me want to hurt you in the same way, just so I could stop feeling so damn much."

"And you did," she whispered.

"I know I did, and you'll never know how sorry I am. I lied when I told myself that once I had you, once I seduced you and ruined you and hurt you, your hold on me would finally dissipate. I lied to myself thinking it would put the past to rest and leave me free to live my life." His voice dropped to silence for a moment, the pattering of rain against the windows filling the quiet. "But my plans haven't quite worked out the way I envisioned. The Cate you were before is the same Cate you are now. And even though I've screwed things up and destroyed your trust in me, I can't give you up again. The love I feel for you is real, and I'm going to fight for you. I'm going to fight for us."

"There is no us anymore," she said, the back of her nose pinching with new tears.

"That's why I didn't tell you what I'd done," he said. "I discovered the truth too late, before I had a chance to stop everything I'd put into place, and I've been working like hell ever since to reverse it before you found out."

"But don't you see? It doesn't matter what you do now. It's

what you *did* that has destroyed anything we might have had together."

"But I can fix it, Cate. I swear, I can. I'll make it better. I'll buy it all back, put it all together again. Just marry me. Stay with me. Let me share my life with you."

"But you can't put *me* back together again," she choked. "I've struggled for ten years to feel whole, to move past my scars and all the internal damage my accident caused. And I believed in you, Ethan. I believed you when you said we had a future. But now, I feel like I've been ripped open for a second time. Only this time, it's worse. It hurts more. Can't you see that? How can I possibly trust you after this?"

"I know how betrayal feels, Cate. I've lived it for ten years, and it's miserable. You have to believe me when I tell you how sorry I am that I've done this to you. I made a mistake because I didn't believe in the woman you truly are. I didn't believe in my own memories of you. I didn't trust myself around you, and I needed a way to fight the pain of it."

"Then how can you expect me to love you when even you don't trust yourself?"

"Because I *do* trust myself now. I trust the way I feel about you. And if you become my wife, I swear I'll do everything I can to make you happy. To make you love me." His voice, soft and quiet and careful, held none of the cocky bravado of before. It betrayed the risk he took, the gamble he'd made by placing his heart in her hands. "I know I don't deserve you, but I swear I'll never hurt you again. I'll protect you with my life. Just tell me you'll have me, Cate, and I'll fight the entire world to keep you from ever feeling pain again."

Every word, every confession brought a new twist of misery inside Cate. Her breath couldn't fight its way around the knot of despair crowding her chest and her entire body shook with the pain of rejecting him. "It's not the world that hurt me, Ethan. It was you. What you did, it killed a part of me, the part I'd need to love you again, and I can't..." She bit her lips, blinking back the tears that threatened to overwhelm her resolve. "We've both hurt each other too much. It's obvious you've never forgiven me, and I'm not sure I could ever trust someone who is capable of doing what you've done."

"If you ever cared for me like you said you did, we can get past this."

"No, we can't." She firmed her jaw and spoke to her hands, hoping he'd take her at her word and accept her decision. "I'd have to love you in order for it to work, and I don't. Not anymore. I can't."

"Then don't love me. Caring for me is enough." He strode around the desk and collected her icy hands between his own. "Please, Cate. I can be happy with that."

"No."

He swallowed with difficulty, his eyes searching hers and his grip tightening around her fingers. "Cate," he choked out, "I swear the love I feel can be enough for us both. And in time, perhaps you'd find a way to forgive me. Perhaps if you tried..."

Despair spiraled through Cate, tempting her to relent. She wanted so badly to accept his apology, to forget what he'd done and simply accept the love he offered. But the icy prickling of warning along her skin urged caution. She couldn't bear to court more pain, to always, always doubt his word. She couldn't bear to bury her fears beneath desire, his seeds of resentment and revenge always germinating beneath a soil fraught with wanting.

She couldn't do it. She couldn't trust him again.

So she pulled her hands from his, the sacrifices of her past merging with the heartbreaking certainty of her future. "No. I won't marry you." Her fingernails dug painfully against her palms. "I won't marry without trust and I can't trust you again. Ever."

"You can't or you won't?" The question, soft with regret, abraded her skin and made her flinch. But the vulnerable pain lacing his voice made her throat constrict, as well. She knew what he wanted. What he needed. He needed a woman who could love him without reservation, a woman who would never hurt him or reject him. He needed a partner he trusted and who trusted him, a soul mate, a woman who shared his goals, his dreams and his future. Once, she'd dreamed of being that woman. But no longer.

Her dreams had died this morning, beneath the harsh pummeling of truth.

"I'm sorry, Ethan, but I won't," she said.

"So we're through?"

"Yes. This isn't about what we've done to each other or the pain we've endured. It's about the way you view me. And the way you view yourself. You may have climbed the ranks in everyone else's eyes and amassed a fortune too large to ever spend, but to yourself, you're still that same boy who was forbidden to speak to me. You'll always feel like you have to prove something, and then you'll lash out when your perceptions of yourself don't change."

"But your love has changed those perceptions."

She shook her head. "No. If it had, we wouldn't be here now. I can't fix how you feel when you're with me and you will always resent me for it. We'd forever be stuck with this huge, insurmountable obstacle that you've shown yourself incapable of moving past." Though she knew it was the only thing she could say to convince him, the words tasted like ash in her mouth. "We don't belong together," she said raggedly. "We never did. You know that."

"No, I don't," he rasped. "After these past weeks, after all we've done together, I don't. You gave me your virginity, for God's sake. You let me touch you and hold you and you can't tell me it meant nothing to you. I won't believe that."

"Of course it meant something to me." She forced the words through a throat gone tight with sorrow. "But that doesn't change who we are. It doesn't mean we can be together."

His fingers threatened to crush the fragile bones of her shoulders. Taking a steadying breath, he lowered his forehead against hers. "Cate," he whispered, his pride wavering like a tangible offering of alms between them. "Don't do this. Please. I can't chart a future without you in it. I won't know who I am."

Her eyes stung, her throat convulsed spasmodically and she could no longer stem the flood of her tears. They slid down her cheeks, burning tracks of pain and remorse along her jaw and neck. She jerked away from his grip, when all she wanted to do was burrow into his warmth and hold his sweet mouth to hers. "You'll find someone," she said in a quavering voice. "Someone whole who loves you, a healthy woman who makes you happy and whom you can treat as an equal. You'll be grateful I didn't accept this reckless proposal of yours and that you won't have to forever live with the memory of the pain we've caused each other."

His jaw hardened and he dipped his head. He stood in silent contemplation for several long, weighted moments before he again lifted his gaze to hers. The desolate sheen in his eyes sent a chill through her, and she realized that his rejected love would soon reclaim its previous icy veneer of hatred.

A hatred she knew would never dissipate, she thought bleakly, averting her eyes.

He inhaled and stepped back, creating even more space in the growing gap of coldness between them. They stood that way, the brittle silence broken only by the hushed murmurings of the rain, until Cate mustered her courage and lifted her gaze to his once more. She couldn't see the exotic blue of his eyes, only the glittering black of his pupils. He looked pale and grim in the dim light, his typical vitality tempered by bleak, embittered acceptance.

She threaded her fingers together at her waist and swallowed thickly. "Please know that I only want you to be happy," she finally whispered.

He didn't move so much as an eyelash. "Right."

Additional beats of silence, an oppressive mantle of despair that nearly bowed her shoulders with its weight, pressed down on her. "I think you'd better go," she told him. Awkwardly, Cate offered her hand.

He acted as if he didn't see the gesture.

Self-conscious and clumsy, she felt her hand start to tremble. She pulled it back, but he caught it before it reached her waist, and brought the back of her hand to his lips. The heat of his mouth against her skin made her knees weaken. "Goodbye, Cate," he whispered.

Her throat narrowed and a wintry shiver stole over her limbs as he released her wrist. She closed her fingers and brought her knotted fist to her ribs. Pressing hard, harder, as if she could relieve some of the pain that gathered within, she turned blindly as the old ache of her injuries rose up from deep within her bones.

CHAPTER FIFTEEN

ETHAN left without being aware of the rain, fury and grief descending upon him like a suffocating mantle from which there was no escape. He wanted to rage at the sky, to sprint back to Cate and convince her she was wrong, that he'd changed. Failing that, he wanted to beat his fists until they bled against the black marble and glass that now belonged to him.

But it was over. He'd gambled his heart and lost.

He entertained a fleeting thought of walking out into the cold embrace of the storm until he reached the sea and its cruel undertow. He wanted to be sucked out to the merciless, yawning maw of nothingness. To stop feeling so damn much.

Black misery swamped his chest, making it hard to breathe. Great, gulping sobs fought for release, but he swallowed back the urge to weep, grimly mustering the control he'd honed for ten interminable years. He waited until the lights of Cate's office turned dark against her windows before slowly, painfully making his way back to the car.

He made it two miles before he had to pull off to the side of the road. For several long moments, he stared unseeing out into the black night until, shaking, he lowered his forehead to his whitened knuckles and wept.

Cate didn't really remember the next twenty-four hours. She spent most of it curled up in her childhood bed, miserably weeping until her eyes burned and breathing became a chore. The words they'd exchanged had annihilated what remained of her composure, and she fervently hoped to never see him again. She doubted she could keep herself from throwing herself at his feet, wailing out her forgiveness. Begging to recant her words, to accept him and love him, no matter the hurt of their past.

Though her decision had been for the best, she couldn't stop reliving the pain in his eyes. She knew the truth had wounded him in a way that was sure to leave yet another layer of deep, abiding scars. The grief and remorse that accompanied the knowledge that she'd caused him pain yet again, no matter whether he deserved it or not, had no outlet. She'd wrung herself dry, and yet the pain remained.

By the next morning, she realized that she would live the rest of her days in coldness. No amount of time could chase the chill away. So she cranked up her radiator, burrowed beneath a pile of thick quilts and stared numbly out at the gray sea.

She dozed fitfully until her back ached from being in one position for so long, until the glow of sunlight replaced the filtered light of dawn. A rattle at her door disturbed her sleep and she sat up blearily, staring at the twisting doorknob. She'd barely wiped aside the cobwebs of sleep when Mrs. Bartholomew, laden with a steaming tray, banged the door open and strode to glare down at Cate as if she'd disappointed her greatly. "Enough, Cate."

"Leave me alone," Cate said with a disoriented grimace, lifting the blanket to her chin and flopping back onto her side.

Mrs. Bartholomew flipped on an overhead lamp, flooding the cold room with brittle light. "You've moped enough, and I won't tolerate any more of it. You need to eat."

"I'm not hungry."

"Too bad." She stood over Cate with a frown. "Death looks better than you."

"Thanks a lot," she said wryly. "I feel like death, too, and if you don't mind, I'd like to go back to sleep. I'm tired."

"If the condition of your clothing and hair is any indication, you've already slept too much."

"So? It's not like I have anything better to do."

"I've supported you through a lot of foolishness, Cate, but this just takes the cake."

"I'm living my life the only way I know how," she shot back with a flare of annoyance. "And I'm sorry if it doesn't fit with your approval."

Mrs. Bartholomew waited a beat before answering, her mouth pulled into an irritated moue. "No, you're not. You're wallowing."

"What do you expect? Am I supposed to go merrily along my way, alone and childless and betrayed by the only man I've ever loved?"

"I expect you to act like a grown woman, instead of throwing away your best chance at happiness."

Cate shook her head, her throat going tight and her chest feeling as though it was too narrow to draw breath. "I don't want to talk about it."

"Too bad."

"Go away."

"No. I let you have it your way before, and I'll be damned if I let you make another stupid decision about that boy." She raised a pointed finger and skewered Cate with a slate-eyed glare. "You made a mistake ten years ago when you lied to Ethan and sent him away. I watched you grieve the loss of your best friend and limp along with your wounded heart, all so you could give Ethan what you thought he wanted. I watched you become reckless with your own life and your own safety because of it. I watched you nearly die. And I'm not willing to go through that again. I won't."

"I'm not asking you to."

"I stood by you for years while you relearned how to walk. And for what? So both you and Ethan could remain miserable and alone?"

"Ethan won't be alone for long. He'll get what he wants."

"He wants you."

"No, he doesn't."

"I saw his face when he brought you all those gifts. Being with you lit him up inside, and nothing you say will convince me otherwise."

"If he wanted me, he wouldn't have betrayed me the way he has."

"Don't you think he thought the very same thing about you? You made a mistake that just about killed him. And he's made one now. It doesn't mean you can't forgive each other and move on."

"Yes, it does," she insisted, her throat thickening with defensive tears. "Neither of us trusts the other. How can we move on from that?"

"When are you going to understand, Cate? Life is never perfect. You work through mistakes and betrayals and pain to make it that way."

Cate looped her arms over her bent legs and knotted her fingers against her shins. Staring down at her whitened knuckles, she said, "I can't forgive him."

"He forgave you."

She lifted her gaze to Mrs. Bartholomew's, ruthlessly crushing the feeble agreement that stirred within her chest. "I didn't hurt him out of hatred and revenge. I hurt him because I loved him."

"Pain is pain, sweetie, no matter the reason behind it."

Frustrated, muddled and feeling backed into a corner, Cate firmed her jaw and argued, "No, it isn't."

Mrs. Bartholomew released a gusty sigh. "For heaven's sake, Cate, he made a mistake. Just like you did. And I'll bet my right arm he's working to repair the damage. Isn't he?"

"Yes," Cate mumbled.

"So why should you be allowed to carry a grudge when he isn't?"

A spark of irritation flared to life, sharpening Cate's tone. "This isn't a grudge!" she blurted. "Nothing would please me more than for him to find happiness and peace."

"If that isn't a pack of lies, I don't know what is." Mrs. Bartholomew shot her a speaking glance. "Your entire life, you've been the one with the power. Oh, you're a fine princess, kind and generous to a fault, and not a soul could ever doubt the goodness of your heart. But other than your father, God rest his soul, people are always left feeling a bit lacking around you."

"What a terrible thing to say!"

"It's not terrible, sweetie. It's just the truth, and Ethan's been doing his best to navigate it for years."

"Ruining Carrington Industries is his best?"

Mrs. Bartholomew shrugged an unconcerned shoulder. "He hasn't done anything that can't be undone."

"That's not the point."

"You're right. The point is that he loves you and you love him. Nothing else matters."

"You're wrong."

"Why?"

She bit her lower lip. Hard. Until the pain of her lip eclipsed the pain squeezing against her lungs. "Because."

Mrs. Bartholomew's expression softened and she joined Cate on the wide bed. "Give him another chance, sweetheart. I'm not saying it'll be easy, but you're strong enough to handle it."

Cate's eyes blurred as she felt Mrs. Bartholomew's soft, warm arm settle over her shoulders. The back of her nose burned. Her heart burned. Everything burned as she realized she'd rejected Ethan's love because she was afraid. She'd wounded the man she loved because she was too scared to take a risk.

Mrs. Bartholomew reached into her pocket for her ever-present supply of tissues. "Here," she said, shoving a wad toward Cate. "Use this before you get snot all over your great-grandmother's handmade quilts."

Cate straightened, dabbing at her running nose and eyes with the tissues. She felt horribly raw, as if she teetered on a tightrope over a forest of sharpened spikes. "I'm scared."

"Of course you are. But if you let fear rule your life, you'll never be happy."

Closing her eyes, Cate felt anxiety well within her chest. Anxiety and a paralyzing fear. As much as she wished to deny it, she knew she'd never be able to fill the gaping hole Ethan's absence would leave behind. Watching him meet and wed and love another would kill her by slow degrees. "Don't you ever get tired of being right?"

"Never." Mrs. Bartholomew smiled, then leaned to offer a squeezing hug. "Go to him, for God's sake. Put all of us out of our misery."

Cate had never been to Ethan's temporary New York office before, and when she entered the giant glass-and-chrome space, the severe elegance of its lines made her wonder if he ever experienced any softness in his life anymore. She stepped through the twelve-foot glass doors and stood, silent and un-noticed, while burly moving men scurried from one room to another toting boxes. Her resolve wavered, urging her to abandon this crazy plan and escape with her dignity intact.

They were readying the office for its transfer back to London, she rationalized. They were busy. He'd be busy. He wouldn't wish to see her again, not after the way she'd rejected him. Again.

But then she saw him through the slightly opened door of his personal office and she knew she'd always regret it if she didn't at least try.

She watched as he appeared and disappeared, pacing before a giant, sleek desk that dominated a room encased in chrome, black-stained mahogany and rippled glass blocks. She couldn't make out his exact words, his voice muffled by the thick gray carpet and panels of glass, but she could see that he was angry. He barked something into his phone, then clicked it shut with a scowl. Turning on his heel, he shoved the cell phone in his pocket and lifted his eyes.

Their gazes collided and she watched him recoil as if he'd been struck. Nervous and scared, she tried to move toward him, but her feet wouldn't move. Her rebellious muscles refused to heed her frantic orders. So she remained frozen while her heart beat painfully against her ribs and her tongue stuck to the roof of her mouth.

Ethan was not as incapacitated as she. His door was ripped aside with a violence that drew a gasp from Cate, and he stormed toward her with fury twisting his mouth into a scowl. Panicked, she braced herself for his anger, curling inward as he drew close.

He bent to grasp her arm as if he were expecting her to flee. The tight grip of his fingers dug into the flesh of her upper arm, making her wince. Cate dared to meet his gaze, thinking she hardly recognized this angry stranger glowering down at her. Looking at him now, she would have never believed he'd once held her, kissed her and pleasured her with such gentle care as he had.

"Why the hell are you here, Cate?" he asked, his harsh words abrading her cowering heart. He lowered his voice and ground out, "Wasn't one afternoon of 'you're never going to change and we have no future' enough?"

"No," she blurted, then quickly shook her head. "I mean yes. I mean—" She stopped talking and inhaled, choosing her words with care. "I was wrong."

He shoved her back, releasing her as if the mere touch of her arm repulsed him. "About what?"

"About us." She moved forward, stopping just shy of touching him, and tipped her face to peer into his wintry eyes. "I forgive you."

Though she'd not thought it possible, his expression became even more closed and remote. "I'm not interested in your forgiveness anymore."

"I forgive you anyway."

Ethan's expression hardened as he stared at her. As inscrutable as always, his face gave no hints as to his feelings or thoughts. Worried he'd toss her out bodily, Cate searched frantically for the correct words, the perfect combination of syllables to make him soften. To make him hear. But then she saw the tic of his pulse just beneath his jaw and its violent beat sent a rush of hope through her. She may have killed his love for her, he might wish her gone, but her presence unnerved him. Regardless of the mask of indifference he'd donned, she affected him.

Cognizant of the way her words had battered his pride, she mustered her courage and offered him her own to flay. Vulnerable, scared and completely at his mercy, she implored, "I know you're probably thinking it's just me being charitable, but it's not."

Yet another silence unfurled between them, Ethan's jaw so

tight that the muscles in his neck twitched. "Damn it, Cate," he finally breathed, his shoulders lowering a fraction.

Dizzying relief spun through her. "Do you have someplace private we could talk?"

"My office." He turned on his heel and strode away from her.

They reached the threshold of Ethan's office and she scurried in after him before drawing to a stumbling halt. Bare nails gave mute evidence to the artwork that had once hung along the walls, while deep dents in the carpet belied the previous position of various chairs. The room was empty, save for the plush carpet, the wide desk and two walls of shuttered windows.

Ethan didn't slow until he reached the half-closed mahogany shutters, his broad back as tense and welcoming as a wall of granite. Silence descended, thick and heavy, as Cate slowly moved toward him. Uncomfortable, nervous and wretchedly afraid now that the moment was here, Cate worried that she'd only muck things up further, that her bumbling words would solicit only more anger.

As if divining her wavering resolve, Ethan turned to face her with a scowl. "What changed your mind?"

Stalling for time, Cate backtracked to the door and turned the lock with a soft click. "I have a confession to make." She turned to face him, her hands gripping the handle of his door at the base of her spine. Cate couldn't contain her nervousness. Violent shivers claimed her limbs, making her teeth chatter. She clenched her jaw and relaxed her hands, forcing herself to walk back to the center of the cavernous office.

After an interminable pause, Ethan stepped grimly toward her, his icy glare upping the tension that pervaded the air. "I'm listening."

Cate couldn't think. Despite her rehearsed explanation, despite her carefully planned words, her mind was blank.

Scared witless, she nervously bit her lip while blinking away a sudden sting of tears.

Ethan's focus dipped to her mouth, and his nostrils flared on an inhale. "Damn it, Cate, out with it already."

Cate dropped her gaze, too much a coward to meet his eyes. She inhaled. Exhaled. And then stacked her hands against her abdomen while speaking to the floor. "I lied to you, too, Ethan. I still love you. I don't trust you, but I love you. I always have. With all my heart. And I'm willing to try again if you are." She closed her eyes, fear winnowing through her. "And I'm sorry about what I said earlier. I don't just want you to be happy. I want to be happy, too." Her stomach quivered beneath her palms as she confessed, "I've discovered I'm miserable without you, so I'm willing to risk being unhappy *with* you if it means we have the chance to be happy together."

The muffled sounds beyond Ethan's door blended with the silence, dropping in volume until there was no sound in the room beyond the beating of her pulse. She inhaled, feeling raw and scared and exposed. Knowing full well that her admission had made her vulnerable in a way she'd never been before, she couldn't bear to meet his eyes. With a single, curt word, he could annihilate her, and the knowledge terrified her.

Ethan made a suffocated sound and moved toward her, breathing as if someone had knocked the wind out of him. "You love me?"

The tortured question caused her chest to tighten painfully. "Yes," she mumbled desolately.

Ethan leaned forward, his anger now tempered by anguish. "Of course I'm willing to risk it, Cate." His trembling hands cradled her cheeks, his glittering eyes wet and grieving. "You're a part of me," he confessed raggedly. "The best part. And I want to spend the rest of my life convincing you of that fact."

Obviously, he didn't understand why she was scared.

Gripping his wrists, she inhaled sharply and blinked hard. "It's not going to be easy."

He glared at her with fervent concern. "Who the hell wants easy?" He dragged a thumb over her quivering lower lip. "I want you, Cate. Easy. Hard. Happy. Scared. I don't care, as long as I have you."

Feebly, Cate twisted her face from his hands and stepped sideways, trying to gain space to think. "We'll probably fight, and disappoint each other on occasion, and you know with my accident, I won't be able to have children. You might regret being with a woman who is damaged, a woman who can't give you sons."

He cursed under his breath and tracked her retreat, reaching to grip her head between his wide, warm palms. Tipping her throat back, he forced her to meet his eyes. Savage, ardent intensity colored his voice. "I've wanted you for my whole life, and I've lived in unrelenting torment because I thought I could never have you. I love you for a million reasons that are anything but easy. I want you simply because you're you. Flawed, imperfect, scarred, damaged, I don't care. I love *you*. I want to spend my days and nights and all the minutes in between with you. I want you at my side at all those awful charity functions, I want you when your hair is messy, when you cry at a romantic movie and when you're too tired to make love. I love your face, your humor, your smiles, the way you care for others and how you somehow manage to be both feminine and strong. Damn it, Cate, don't you see that? If I have you, then we can work through everything else." He stopped to suck in a breath, his bleak eyes as tormented as those of a condemned man. "Cate," he whispered, "don't you know what my life is like without you in it?"

"I do." Tears overflowed, trailing messy wetness down her cheeks. "It's mine without you."

"No. It's worse. Because I broke your trust in my love.

And because of it, I almost condemned us both to a lifetime of pain." His mouth twisted in agony. "I'm so sorry, Cate."

"It's okay." Her voice broke. "I'm sorry, too."

"You're forgiven." He slanted his damp mouth over hers, assaulting her with rough, feverish kisses. "You're my soul," he breathed against her skin, dragging his lips to her chin, her cheeks, her brow. "Every day I've had to live without you has been hell. Every woman I've tried to replace you with has been wrong, each one more unsatisfying than the last—"

"Don't—" she moaned.

"But I couldn't stop," he continued savagely, "because I needed something to stop the memory of you in my arms. I've had no peace, no rest. No matter where I turn, it's you. *You*, Cate." He broke off to devour her with raw, ravenous kisses. The taste of their mingled tears made Cate shudder with heat. Disoriented and reeling, she trembled beneath the jolts of pleasure his touch ignited. Ethan held her with a passion tinged with violence, his chest moving in hard, shallow breaths and his fingers gripping with enough force to leave bruises on her sensitive flesh. "Jesus," he blurted, with the exasperation of a man who'd suffered beyond his ability to endure. "Do you know what these last few days have been like? You've put me through hell, Cate."

Suddenly, Cate felt his arms across her back and upper thighs. Before she realized what had happened, he'd lifted her within his arms and spun toward his desk. "Ethan!" she squeaked.

"Hush. We're just going to make love."

Dangling over his arms, her linen skirt rucked high against her thighs and one shoe already gone, Cate squirmed to reclaim her dignity. "No! We're in your office! Please. There are people, your employees for God's sake, right outside that door!"

"Then we'd better be quiet, don't you think?"

"I can't," she answered frantically. "Everything's happening too fast. We still haven't discussed—"

"Cate," he interrupted tightly, "I don't give a damn about who does or doesn't hear, and I'm done talking. I'm making love to you now, and nothing is going to stop me."

Shaking, Cate felt a resurgence of heat claim her limbs. "But—"

"Shh." Ethan dipped his head to brush his mouth over hers. "We can be quiet," he whispered. "I promise."

She shivered in nervous denial. She worried that she couldn't contain her response, should he truly make love to her here. In public. After a lifetime of behaving as she should, always aware of her place in society and the expectation that she maintain appearances, she couldn't help it. But the knowledge that nothing she said would sway his decision made her pulse thrash crazily as he strode toward his desk. Reaching its polished length, he lowered her buttocks to the cool, wide surface. As she regained her balance, her palms coming into contact with the sleek mahogany, he stepped between her thighs and claimed her mouth anew.

Much, much later, after he'd made exquisitely silent love to her, Cate's limbs felt too heavy to move. Draped around him, her cheek pressed against his sweat-filmed chest, she closed her eyes. "I love you, Ethan."

"I love you, too, Catydid." His heartbeat gradually slowed as he smoothed her damp hair back from her face and off her neck. His voice dipped low as he bent to kiss her forehead. "Always."

EPILOGUE

Two years later

"It'll be okay," Ethan said, looking down at her with poorly-disguised worry tightening his features. "You're just exhausted. Between the move and all our travel this past year, it's no wonder you're so tired. It's nothing a good rest won't cure."

Cate, garbed in a paper gown and shivering beneath two rows of harsh fluorescent lights, stared wordlessly at the diagrams on her doctor's wall, her mind whirling with worst-case scenarios. Dr. Slattery had been out of the room for nearly an hour. Surely it didn't take that long to run a couple of tests, did it?

"Cate."

She looked at Ethan, at the concern that pulled at his strained smile of encouragement, and tried to muster matching optimism. It didn't work. She was scared. So scared that her hands were numb and her teeth clacked together.

Ethan moved to cup her face between his palms, then leaned to press a comforting kiss against her chilled lips. "It'll be okay, Cate. Whatever it is, it'll be okay. We'll fight it together."

A slight rap on the door had both Cate and Ethan stiffening.

Ethan's hand dropped to hers as he turned to face the news of their future.

Dr. Slattery bustled in, dragging an ultrasound machine and shaking his head. "Well, I've run the tests three times and I keep getting the same result." He lifted the lab papers between them, as if the maze of letters and numbers would make sense to either of them.

"What is it?" Ethan asked, worry lending urgency to his tone.

"I have to check one more thing before I can tell you for sure." Dr. Slattery moved to place a hand on Cate's shoulder. "We need to do an ultrasound. Are you okay with that?"

Cate nodded and slowly lay back on the examining table, trying to make her mind go blank. *Don't borrow trouble*, she thought, just as Mrs. Bartholomew would advise. But when Dr. Slattery spread the cold gel on her abdomen and aligned the hated ultrasound wand over her abdomen, she felt her world narrow. Blackness encroached on the edges of her vision while her heart thrashed violently in her chest. What if her internal wounds had caused new complications to develop? She closed her eyes, not wanting to see the evidence of more tragedy on the grainy screen.

Soon, the silence in the small room gave way to the familiar shushing sound of the machine. Dr. Slattery cocked his head and moved the wand farther down, transcribing a slow, circular arc over her lower abdomen.

Cate pressed her cheek against the paper lining of the padded table and tried not to cry. She didn't want to know what was wrong. Not yet. She wanted to pretend everything was okay for a little while longer. She wanted to savor her time with Ethan, to continue enjoying the lovely marriage they'd built together. Things were perfect. She didn't want her stupid body or its flaws to change things.

"Well, Cate, it looks like the tests were right," the doctor said.

Cate felt Ethan tense beside her and then his big body pressed against her side as he leaned forward to see. "What?" His low voice was a strained whisper. "What is it?"

"It's impossible, that's what it is." The doctor angled the ultrasound wand until a new rhythm, rapid and faint, unfurled in the small room.

Cate's eyes flew open while Ethan's grip upon her icy fingers tightened. "Doctor?"

Dr. Slattery's round face pleated in a smile. "You're pregnant, Cate."

"What?" they blurted in unison.

"It looks like you're about twelve weeks along."

Ethan stared at the doctor in a shocked silence that mirrored her own. "But we thought… How…?"

Dr. Slattery's smile deepened. "I imagine it happened the usual way."

Ethan's stunned gaze drifted to hers while Cate's hands lifted to hover over her exposed abdomen. "But we were told," she said before shifting her focus back to Dr. Slattery. "*You* told us we wouldn't be able to conceive."

"I know." Dr. Slattery lifted both palms as he shrugged. "I guess nature had a different plan."

"But you were the fifth doctor to give us the same opinion. How could all of you be wrong?"

Again, he shrugged. "Bodies don't always behave the way we think they will. Sometimes, that one in a million chance pays off and everyone gets surprised." He smiled as he offered Cate a paper towel to wipe her belly. "I'd say this little tyke wants to be in the world so much, he's willing to fight the odds."

She and Ethan exchanged a glance and then turned back to the doctor. "He?"

"You might want to start investing in blue."

"It's a miracle," Cate breathed.

"No." Ethan turned shining eyes to Cate, a slow smile claiming his mouth. "*You're* the miracle."

Cate's trembling lips curved while dizzying happiness winged through her chest. She reached blindly for Ethan's hand and then pulled it to her lips. Blinking through her tears, she kissed his palm and then moved it lower to press his long fingers against her belly. "You're going to be a father, Ethan."

"A father to our baby. Ours, Cate." His cheek creased with the dimple she'd never stopped loving. "And I can't imagine loving our son's mother any more than I do right now."

MODERN

THE MARRIAGE BETRAYAL
by Lynne Graham
Sander Volakis has no intention of marrying—until he sees Tally Spencer. He can't resist her...little knowing that one night with the innocent Tally could end his playboy existence...

Doukakis's Apprentice
by Sarah Morgan
Wanted: willing apprentice to handle incorrigible, womanising (but incredibly sexy) tycoon! Polly Prince is determined to make a lasting success of the position, but soon learns that her workaholic boss *can* put pleasure before business!

Heart of the Desert
by Carol Marinelli
One kiss is all it takes for Georgie to know Sheikh Ibrahim is trouble, Trapped in the swirling sands, she surrenders to the rebel Prince—yet the law of his land decrees that she can never really be his...

Her Impossible Boss
by Cathy Williams
Successful New Yorker Matt Strickland's sexiness is off the scale, but new employee, feisty nanny Tess Kelly, thinks his capacity for fun definitely shows room for improvement! Although he's *determined* to keep things professional...

MODERN

THE ICE PRINCE
by Sandra Marton

No opponent can penetrate Prince Draco Valenti's icy exterior…except high-flying, straight-talking lawyer Anna Orsini! They're at odds in business, but in the bedroom Draco's desire for Anna has the power to melt *all* his defences!

SURRENDER TO THE PAST
by Carole Mortimer

Mia Burton thinks she's seen the last of Ethan Black—the man who haunts her heart. But Ethan's returned in all his very real glory, and it's clear he'll do *whatever* it takes to win her back!

RECKLESS NIGHT IN RIO
by Jennie Lucas

Gabriel Santos offers Laura Parker a million dollars to pretend she loves him. But they've already shared one unforgettable night in Rio, and Gabriel's not aware he's the father of Laura's baby…

THE REPLACEMENT WIFE
by Caitlin Crews

Theo Markou Garcia needs a wife—or someone who looks like his infamous fiancée—so offers disowned Becca Whitney a deal: masquerade as the Whitney heiress in exchange for her own true fortune…but don't fall for her husband!

On sale from 1st July 2011
Don't miss out!

Available at WHSmith, Tesco, ASDA, Eason and all good bookshops

www.millsandboon.co.uk

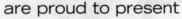

Discover Pure Reading Pleasure with

MILLS &
BOON

**Visit the Mills & Boon website for all
the latest in romance**

- 🌹 **Buy** all the latest releases, backlist and eBooks

- 🌹 **Find out** more about our authors and their books

- 🌹 **Join** our community and chat to authors and other readers

- 🌹 **Free** online reads from your favourite authors

- 🌹 **Win** with our fantastic online competitions

- 🌹 **Sign** up for our free monthly eNewsletter

- 🌹 **Tell us** what you think by signing up to our reader panel

- 🌹 **Rate** and review books with our star system

www.millsandboon.co.uk

 Follow us at twitter.com/millsandboonuk

 Become a fan at facebook.com/romancehq

NEATH PORT TALBOT LIBRARY
AND INFORMATION SERVICES

1	419	25		49		73	
2		26		50		74	
3		27		51		75	
4		28		52		76	
5		29		53		77	
6		30		54		78	
7	5720	31		55		79	
8		32		56		80	
9		33		57		81	
10		34		58		82	
11		35		59		83	
12		36		60		84	
13		37		61		85	
14		38		62		86	
15		39		63		87	
16		40		64	11/14	88	
17		41		65		89	
18		42		66		90	
19		43		67		91	
20		44		68		92	
21		45		69		COMMUNITY SERVICES	
22		46		70			
23		47		71		NPT/111	
24		48		72			